T0245739

The Age of Amy

MAD DOGS & MAKEOVERS

BY BRUCE EDWARDS

Lambert Hill

Lambert Hill
P.O. Box 1478
Brea, CA 92822-1478
www.LambertHill.com

The Age of Amy: Mad Dogs and Makeovers
Copyright © 2016 by Bruce Edwards

All rights reserved.

This is a work of fiction. Names, characters, places, and incidents
either are the product of the author's imagination or are used
fictitiously. Any resemblance to actual persons, living or dead,
events, or locales is entirely coincidental.

No part of this publication may be reproduced, or stored in a
retrieval system, or transmitted in any form, or by any means,
electronic, mechanical, photocopying, recording, or otherwise,
without written permission of the publisher. For information
regarding permissions: Lambert Hill, P.O. Box 1478, Brea, CA
92822. Books@LambertHill.com.

ISBN: 9780983760498 (Print)
ISBN: 9780692541159 (E-book)

www.AgeOfAmy.com

The Age of Amy Books

Bonehead Bootcamp

"Truly a book about finding one's real self."
—*All Books Review*

The Thumper Amendment

"Readers will appreciate Amy's sharp wit."
—*Booklist*

Channel '63

"A riotous young-adult adventure."
—*Foreword Reviews*

Behind the Fun Zone

"Entertaining read from beginning to end."
—*Midwest Book Review*

Theme Farm Collection
BOX SET
BOOKS 1-3

Bonehead Bootcamp
The Thumper Amendment
Channel '63

To
ROD SERLING

Whose own magic mirrors
reflected our true nature.

Contents

Chapter 1

Are You Watching?

*L*et's call him Policeman #1. I had forgotten the officer's name the moment he said it. And why wouldn't I? It's not every day that the Law comes knocking at your door. I spied the man on my front porch through the peep hole and thought, What have I done wrong now?

True, I was known for being somewhat of a trouble-maker, but I never raised a stink that wasn't justified. So, what was I worried about? I mean, the cops wouldn't haul an innocent 16-year-old girl off to jail for no reason, would they?

The porch light lit up one side of the man's face, while the other side faded into the night. He seemed harmless enough.

I opened the door to find a short, portly gentleman in a white shirt and thin black tie, wearing a Shankstonville Police Department windbreaker. He politely removed his cap and asked, "is this the

Dawson residence?"

There was a time when officers of the law had that macho look—lean and hunky, with a mustache that matched the curve of their teardrop shades. I was a city girl back then, and like most adolescent females, I viewed policemen as brave and incredibly sexy. Lawmen in the farming community where I now lived didn't quite fit that city cop mold, especially with their expanding waistlines.

"I'd like to speak with the head of the household, please," said the officer.

Hearing the voice of our unexpected visitor, my dad bounded up beside me. "That would be me, sir," he said. "What brings you out this way?"

A good question. Our upscale neighborhood seldom required the need for law enforcement. Every home was equipped with the most up-to-date, hi-tech security systems available. We had more surveillance cameras on our block than the Federal Reserve building in Washington D.C.

"Who's at the door, honey?" called my mom, shuffling across our marble entryway in her flip-flops.

"Sorry to bother you at this late hour, ma'am," said the officer. "Hope I didn't intrude on your dinner."

Another policeman, this one taller and much, much thinner, paraded up our walkway like a military general. Under his jacket was a service

2

revolver, tucked in a shoulder holster. He stood at attention behind his partner, then said, in a deep baritone voice, "Ma'am . . . Sir . . . Miss."

We'll call him Policeman #2.

"If it's convenient," said #1, "we'd like to have a word with Amy."

Amy! Hearing my name gave me the heebie-jeebies right down to my toes. My dad, who was well aware of the mischief I was capable of, looked down at me sharply.

I tipped my head back, and with puppy dog eyes, whimpered, "I'm innocent!"

My playful remark broke the tension, and showed that I wasn't always so serious about everything. Just because I was politically active, people figured I didn't have a sense of humor. But, I didn't care. If there was a protest march against some social injustice, I was in it. If an anti-war movement needed volunteers to gather signatures, count me in. My only activity that didn't raise eyebrows was my charitable work for *The Wild Things Survival Fund*—an animal rights group. Last I heard, stuffing donation envelopes and serving coffee at fundraisers was not a criminal offense.

"Forgive me," said #1. "I didn't mean to suggest that your daughter had broken the law. We've been tracking a suspicious man who we haven't been able to identify. He made a phone call this evening that was traced to Amy's cell phone."

"Sounds like a computer glitch," said Dad. "The only suspicious calls we get here are pranks from Amy's friends."

"Maybe that's all it was, but we'd still like to ask her a few questions."

My mom swung the door open. "Won't you come in?"

"Not so fast!" I said. "Isn't someone going to check their ID?"

Dad laughed nervously. "Amy, you're embarrassing these gentlemen."

#1 raised his hand. "No problem."

The men held out their identification cards. I studied each one closely. They didn't look much different than common drivers licenses, with profile photos and signatures.

"How do we know these are even real?" I said. "Have you ever seen a police ID before? Anyone could fake one in Photoshop, print it, put it in a fancy sleeve, and claim to be a cop."

Dad grinned impishly at the officers, then said apologetically, "She's at that age."

"Dad!" I cried. "You're not going to let total strangers into our house, are you? They've got guns!"

My appeal for caution, which seemed perfectly reasonable to me, was ignored. The officers were graciously ushered into the living room. Then I noticed that #1 wasn't a local policeman at all, but a federal agent. *FBI* in bold letters spread across the back of his jacket.

I took the comfy armchair, while the short one faced me from the edge of the coffee table. #2 hovered over him, content to remain standing.

Whipping a notepad and a pen from his shirt pocket, #1 promptly asked me, "Did someone call you earlier this evening?"

"Yes," I said.

"Who was it?"

"I don't know."

"How did he sound?"

"That's hard to say."

"How long did you talk?"

I turned to my dad, sitting wide-eyed on the couch with my mom. "Do I have to do this?"

#2 leaned down over me. "We welcome your full cooperation, miss."

"Don't be afraid, Amy," said Dad. "Just answer the questions as best you can."

I felt like I was standing naked at the center of a three-ring circus. Everyone was staring at me. Something didn't feel right about all this. I couldn't put my finger on what, but I decided to play along for now.

"I didn't talk to my caller very long," I said.

"Tell me everything that happened—from the beginning, please."

"Well, I was alone in my room, reading. I read a

lot. I'm just into my first Agatha Christie mystery: *The Murder of Roger Ackroyd.* You guys know that one, right?"

Two blank stares.

I went on. "Next thing, my cell phone rang. 'Hello,' I said. A voice on the other end—a man's voice I'd never heard before—said, *'Are you watching?'*"

#1's pen point was pressed against his notepad, but hadn't moved an inch. "Aren't you going to write this down?" I asked.

"Not until I hear something relevant. What did he say next?"

"The man told me to turn on the TV news. All the local stations were broadcasting live helicopter video of a police pursuit. The car being chased was one of those humongous pickup trucks everyone drives these days. Then the man said, *'See that black truck? I'm driving it.'* Then he hung up."

"Did he say anything else?"

"That was pretty much it."

Normally, I'm not in the habit of lying, but I had just told one. There was much more to our conversation, but I still had my doubts about those men, and didn't feel comfortable giving them the details.

This is the rest of what the caller and I said to each other:

"Who is this, really?"   *"I told you. I'm the one being chased."*

"Yeah, right! And I'm suppose to believe that?"   *"I'll prove it to you. Watch!"*

The news chopper camera was tight on the driver side window. An arm extended out of it and waved up and down.

"See that? I'm waving to you. Believe me now?"

"I guess I'll have to. But why are you calling me?"   *"I called some others, but no one would talk to me. So, I dialed this number at random."*

If this was a prank, it was a pretty convincing one.

"What's your name?"

This was where I should have hung up, but I figured, how much trouble could this guy make?

"Amy."   *"How old are you?"*

7

| "Sixteen." | *"I have a daughter about your age. She's graduating from high school tomorrow. In fact, this truck is her graduation present."* |

| "Why don't you call her, then?" | *"She was the first one to hang up on me. What's the news saying?"* |

| "That your truck was reported stolen." | *"That's my Debbie! That's my little cherub! She blames me for everything, even the birthmark on her nose--a tiny dot you can hardly notice."* |

| "What's she got against you?" | *"I don't spend enough time with her. I'm way too busy for parenting. Guess I'm not a very good dad."* |

The truck made a hard left, with the police cruisers right on its tail.

"Do you know where you're going?"

"Are you kidding? I grew up in this town. Know it like the back of my hand."

He slowed down as he passed Shankstonville Elementary School.

"This is were I learned to cheat kids out of their lunch money."

He slowed in front of the Shankstonville National Bank.

"This is where I learned how a deliberately misplaced decimal point would put money in my pocket."

He drove past a tall office building.

"I swindled Wall Street investors out of millions here."

Why was this guy telling me all this? I felt like a priest listening to a con artist confess his sins.

"You know you can't get away. These pursuits always end the same, with the driver spread-eagle in the street and guns pointed at his head."

"Who says I want to get away? I've been running all my life, Amy, and I can tell you this: You can escape justice, but you can't outrun your conscience."

Our conversation was getting freakier by the minute. Whatever his issues were, nothing I said could possibly resolve them.

"This all sounds like a matter for the police. Turn yourself in. I'm hanging up now."

"I wish you wouldn't. You're the last person on Earth I'm ever going to talk to."

Shivers ran through my whole body. The man was obviously suicidal. I was in a dangerous position, and had no clue how to handle it.

"What are you planning to do?"

"Two miles down this road--two turns to the left and one to the right--the asphalt turns to gravel. Beyond that is Grand Gorge."

Everyone in Shankstonville knew about "The Gorge." It was our town's most famous natural wonder. Tourists flocked there each year to overlook the three-thousand-foot drop to the canyon floor.

"I told you I know this town."

"I know what you're thinking, and you can't do it!"

"Of course I can. There isn't a wall or a barricade this tank can't crash through."

I was now on my feet, pacing the room, listening to a total stranger preparing to take his own life.

"Sorry I won't get to know you better, Amy. You sound like the daughter I always wanted, but never got."

"Stop! Turn around!"

"I'd really like to oblige you, but I've got a date with the devil."

The phone went silent.

From the edge of my bed, I watched as the pickup accelerated. Dirt spewed from its tires while skidding around road blocks. Fences fell like they were made of popsicle sticks. And as the truck reached the edge of the cliff, the news chopper veered off, sparing viewers the gruesome finale to the dramatic chase. All I saw after that was a brilliant flash against the canyon walls, like exploding fireworks.

Though I kept this information to myself, I really wasn't withholding much more than anyone with a TV didn't already know.

"One final question," said #1. "Did the caller tell you his name?"

"No," I said. "But why ask me? Doesn't your phone-tracking app tell you that?"

"The phone was activated under a bogus name. The truck was brand new, and wasn't registered. We were hoping you could tell us who he was."

"What about DNA testing on the body?"

The pudgy agent stood up and closed his notepad. "That's just it. There is *no* body. When we examined the wreckage, the truck was empty."

"Maybe the man jumped out before he went over the cliff."

"The pursuing officers would have seen it."

"That doesn't make sense. There must be *something* left of him."

"So you would think. Even an explosive crash like that leaves some forensic evidence, but we found nothing. No skeletal remains, no personal effects, no melted credit cards. The fire destroyed his fingerprints if there were any. But we did find *this* on the ground nearby."

He handed me a business card with burn marks around the edges. It read:

Ravi's 2-Bit Solution
Hairstyling and Makeovers

"We've already spoken with the owner," said #2, "He was no more help than you."

"Why don't you keep this card," said #1. "It might help you remember something you may have forgotten."

The interview was over, but I had a few questions of my own. "What did that man do?" I asked. "Why were the police chasing him?"

"He's a suspected terrorist. A suspicious package was found in front of an office building. Eyewitnesses reported seeing a black pickup fleeing the scene. We were after him almost immediately. When he didn't stop, we were sure we had our man. Now, we don't know *what* we have. What worries us is that whoever he is—or was—may still be out there."

"What was in the package?"

"A homemade explosive device. The bomb squad defused it before it went off."

"What kind of maniac would do such a thing?"

"Someone who hates America . . . or hates animals. His target was *The Wild Things Survival Fund*. We

13

know you're a volunteer there, Amy. Strange, that the suspect called *you* of all people, wouldn't you say?"

"Quite a coincidence, isn't it, miss?" added #2.

Mom and Dad walked the officers to the door. The men tipped their caps. "Evening, ma'am. Sir."

The house was dead quiet after the front door closed. My parents' eyes were solidly fixed on me.

I looked back at them timidly. "You don't think *I* had anything to do with this, do you?"

Mom rushed to my side. "Of course not, sweetie. No one's saying you did."

"Don't be ridiculous," said Dad. "Why would you be involved in blowing up the very organization you love working for? Anyway, I wouldn't worry about it." He yawned. "I think I'll turn in."

"Me, too," said Mom.

As they both retired for the night, I sat alone in the quiet. No fingers were pointing at me, yet a dark cloud of suspicion still lingered in the air. That was mostly my fault. With my reputation for stirring things up, why wouldn't the police doubt my sincerity? True, I had a streak of rebellion as plain as the blue streak in my hair, but inferring that I had collaborated with a terrorist was insane! Until I could separate myself from that despicable act, that dark cloud would always follow me.

I knew what I had to do: find that mystery man! But, where to begin?

My clues were a suicide with no body, a terrorist with no name, and a scorched business card from a barbershop. Not much to go on. Still, the idea of playing detective sparked my imagination. Attempting to solve a real-life mystery excited me. It was the opportunity of a lifetime, and a chance for an adventure worthy of Agatha Christie.

Chapter 2

School Daze

"Did you walk the dog?" Asked my father— his voice echoing down the staircase.

"Can you do it, Dad?" I replied. "I'm late for school."

"Need I remind you, Amy? He's *your* dog."

That statement was slightly inaccurate, because that dog really *wasn't* mine—not by choice, anyway. "Scraps" had been my late Aunt Sylvia's dear companion, and her loyal friend in her final days. With my aunt's passing, the fate of her beloved canine created a huge rift within our family. No one wanted to take custody of the little mutt. Driving Scraps to the animal shelter was discussed, even though we all knew it would likely be a one-way trip. Finally, to keep peace in the family—and Scraps alive—I assumed responsibility for him. What else could I do?

To be clear, I have nothing against dogs. I love

all animals. I would never harm a hair, a feather, or a fin of any of God's creatures. I rescued helpless spiders out of bathtubs. Cockroaches had as much right to life as anyone, so long as they lived it outdoors.

The problem was that Scraps wasn't a very desirable pet. No breed would claim him as their own. He was a mix of Poodle, Chihuahua, and the rest was pure guesswork. Not that he was an ugly dog. He was kinda cute, in his own way. But Scraps' affection was reserved for Aunt Sylvia and no one else. Get to close to him and he growls. Try to pet him and he barks. Feed him and he nips at your hand. The only time he wasn't a threat to life and limb was when sleeping in his doggie bed.

7: 23 am

The school year was winding down. Summer recess was right around the corner. There was no homework to turn in, no lectures to sleep through, no math tests to sweat over. Finals had all been graded and report cards delivered to relieved parents. Most of us had already said our farewells to teachers and classmates.

With the warm weather, and barely a week of school left, many kids didn't bother to show up. Traffic in the corridors was lighter than the Interstate on a Sunday morning.

For those of us who slugged it out to the end, the

anticipated summer break was no less enticing. But the real chatter around campus was about an even bigger event. *Z Beanie Run,* the pop music sensation and teenage heartthrob, had announced he would be performing at the county fairgrounds! The thrilling news left schoolgirls breathless and parents terrified. Beanie was far from the ideal teenage role model. His song lyrics were laced with sexual innuendoes and promiscuity. (No wonder he was so popular with the kids!)

Practically overnight, concert flyers littered the school hallways. Posters covered walls and ceilings, all showing the pop star's signature headgear: an old-style beanie with the little propeller on top.

The teen idol stared down on me from a show bill pasted over my locker. I snarled at him before ripping it down. While most girls my age swooned at the mere mention of Beanie's name, I had a hard time getting enthused about him. For sure, he put on a spectacular live show, but buried under all the stage fog, laser lights, and pyrotechnics, there wasn't much worth listening to. That's why I was so surprised to hear a voice behind me ask:

"You going?"

It was Hubert, my special high school buddy.

If I was the poster child for rebellious youth, Hubert was my twin brother. We shared the same concerns over the kind of world our generation would one day inherit. There was nothing we couldn't tell each other, and no topic was off limits. On a personal level, however, our relationship was strictly Platonic. Not that I didn't find Hubert appealing. He had a brilliant mind, winning high honors for his aptitude toward math and science. For sure, he was a card-carrying member of the Nerd Guild, but I enjoyed his company. But there is an unwritten law of nature that says: when intimacy begins, friendships end. Hubert and I were good friends. Nothing more.

Inviting me to a Beanie concert was a bit out of character for Hubert.

"You know me better than that," I told him. "That'll be the day when I pay to see an overrated, auto-tuned juvenile delinquent, dance across a stage with his belt below his butt."

"I just thought that the two of us could go out and have a little fun together, that's all," moaned Hubert.

"You mean, a date?"

"Not a date. Call it . . . a research project."

"Why don't we just call it what it *really* is: a date."

Hubert stared at the ground to hide his embarrassment, "So, what if it is?"

I would sooner cut off my thumbs than hurt Hubert's feelings. The rejected look on his reddened face told me I needed to let him down easy. I didn't exactly say I *wouldn't* go with him, I just said: "Beanie? Are you kidding me?"

"Sorry," said Hubert. "That was a bad idea."

It was a narrow escape, but I had cleverly refused his invitation while preserving our bond of friendship . . . until he said, "How about the Junior Prom, then?"

Another voice entered the conversation: "Why don't you ask *me* to the prom?"

It was another pal of mine, Lydia Hobbs.

Our friendship was even more peculiar. We were once bitter adversaries in the race for our school's Student Body President. Like all political contests, there was plenty of mud-slinging and dirty tricks. Being the most popular girl in school, Lydia was a shoo-in. But knowing how badly I wanted the job, she unselfishly withdrew. We've been buddies ever since.

In all other respects, Lydia and I were polar opposites:

She was creme brulee,

I was apple pie.

She was Sinatra,

I was Clapton.

She was Versace,

I was Levis.

Now, we were rivals in a new competition: which of us would accompany Hubert to the Junior Prom. I wasn't eager for a tug-of-war over Hubert. If he wanted to take her, so be it. I wasn't going to let it bother me. Still, the thought of the two of them together touched a jealous nerve in me I didn't know I had.

"Hold on, Lydia," I said. "I haven't answered Hubert yet."

"So, what are you waiting for?" she said.

"I need time to think it over."

Lydia laughed. "Listen to you. Get asked to a peace rally and you're gone in a flash, but get asked out on a date and you have to think about it."

Hubert's face got redder. "I gotta get to class."

"Don't go yet!" demanded Lydia. "I want you to hear what Amy's going to say next."

Now *I* was blushing. "You think you're so smart," I said. "Well, how is it that the hottest girl at Shankstonville High hasn't been asked to the prom?"

"I've already been asked by dozens of boys," she said. I turned them all down, waiting to hear from Hubert."

It was the old squeeze play. Rejecting Hubert would leave an opening for Lydia to move in, and I couldn't allow that to happen. Just thinking of myself home alone, while they danced together in front of the whole Junior Class, was already raising my blood pressure. Then there was the scandal that would surely follow. I had no choice but to accept Hubert's invitation.

But before I could respond, a light suddenly

came on in Hubert's face. He displayed a sly grin. "Yes, Lydia," he said. "I would be honored to escort you to the prom."

Lydia was tongue-tied—a rare sight to behold. Her attempt to force my hand had backfired.

"Ah, are you s-sure you want to?" she asked Hubert.

"Definitely! I can't wait! We're going to have such a swell time."

"Swell?"

I was ecstatic. The alluring temptress, who could have chosen any boy she wanted, would be attending the prom with our school's ambassador to Dweebland.

Hubert smiled and winked at me, then proudly walked off to class.

"Better bone up on your modern physics," I told Lydia. "Hubert especially likes discussing the laws of thermodynamics."

She turned up her nose. "Oh, I don't know about that. I'll bet Hubert's a completely different guy away from all those libraries and laboratories. Even Einstein had his party animal side. I think I'm going to enjoy this date."

I guess I had that coming, but so what? Turning Hubert down was the right thing to do. On the other hand, it wouldn't have killed me to go out with him. Either way, I saved our friendship.

Or did I? Maybe my arrogance had pushed the

limits of our relationship too far. Maybe that wink was his subtle way of telling me, "You screwed up!"

2: 36 pm

Sitting in half-filled classrooms all day was like serving time in prison: long hours with nothing to do. The ringing of the final bell was like a last-minute pardon from the governor. I was free to go, but I had one stop to make first: Miss Jeffries' science classroom.

Though Science was not my favorite subject, Miss Jeffries was my favorite teacher. I wish I could say that I was her favorite pupil. At times, I could be her worst nightmare—like the time she covered the contributions NASA had made to space exploration. I argued that the billions it costs to send men into space was better spent here on Earth, like for funding homeless shelters and feeding the hungry. She didn't speak to me for a week after that.

But when I fell behind in my grades, Miss Jeffries took time out to tutor me after school—a generous sacrifice for someone on a teacher's salary. Now, I needed to pick her problem-solving brain, in hopes of learning what happened to my mysterious night caller.

"You busy?" I asked, poking my head through the classroom door. Miss Jeffries sat at her desk in the empty room, enjoying an after-school snack. "Sorry. I didn't know you were eating. I'll come back tomorrow."

"No, no," she insisted, "I'm just finishing my leftover salad before it goes bad. Come in."

I sat at a student desk in the front row. "I have a question that needs some scientific elucidation."

"Wherever did you learn a big word like *elucidation?*"

"From you."

"Oh. Okay, what's your question?"

"You know how sometimes people go missing? The police question everybody. Search parties scour the countryside. Reward money is posted for anyone knowing their whereabouts, but they're never found. Now, suppose someone was in a terrible car wreck. He drove off a cliff, let's say. It's a horrific crash. No one could have survived it. The police go down to retrieve the body, but to their astonishment, there's no driver in the car."

"You mean, there *was* a driver. They just can't find him."

"I mean that the driver has physically disappeared, like a missing person that no one ever finds. Vanished! Poof!"

Miss Jeffries bit into a tomato. "Things don't 'poof' in the real world. There's always a reasonable explanation—like, the driver was ejected, or his dead body was dragged off by a hungry bear."

"I understand that. But what's the possibility that he has just ceased to exist, through some strange force we can't comprehend?"

The patient teacher put down her fork and stared at me like I was loony. "You're talking fantasy, Amy."

"Really?" I read from the notes I had jotted down on a 3x5 card:

"In 1937 aviator Amelia Earhart disappeared while flying over the Pacific Ocean. Her body was never recovered. World War II band leader Glenn Miller's plane vanished somewhere over the English Channel. His body wasn't found, either. Similar unexplained disappearances have occurred over the Bermuda Triangle in the Atlantic Ocean. All of these people are officially presumed dead, yet there are groups who insist they were abducted by space aliens."

"Foolish speculation!" huffed Miss Jeffries. "These tragedies were thoroughly investigated, and given the circumstances, it's reasonable to conclude that each of them ended their travels in a watery grave."

"No aliens?"

"No aliens."

"No poof?"

"No poof!"

"Then, how about this: I read where the pilot of a private plane radioed a distress call. The plane later crashed, but when help arrived, there was no body, as if he had beamed aboard the Starship

Enterprise."

"Read a little further. He was later found relaxing on the beach in South America. He faked his own death to get out of paying alimony to his ex-wife."

"No beam me up, Scotty?"

"No beam me up, Scotty."

"No poof?"

"No poof!"

"But what if he *hadn't* turned up? Why wouldn't an alien abduction be just as valid an explanation? I mean, without evidence, how can you be absolutely sure of anything?"

Miss Jeffries picked up a napkin, wadded it into a ball, then stuffed it into her fist. When she opened her hand, the napkin was gone!"

"Hey, cool!" I said. "How'd you do that?"

"A simple parlor trick. Now tell me, did the napkin disappear?"

"It sure looks that way."

She formed a fist again, then pulled the napkin back out of it. "You only assumed it vanished because you don't know the secret to the trick."

Then she plucked a slice of cucumber out of her salad and placed it on the desktop. "Where's the cucumber?"

"On your desk."

She rolled it across the surface like a tire. It fell off the edge onto the floor. "The cucumber is no longer on the desk. Did it disappear? No. It's been relocated. That's a *reasonable* assumption. Understand?"

"Perfectly," I said. "But I also understand that *un*reasonable assumptions aren't necessarily *un*true. You yourself teach how people laughed at Galileo for believing that the Earth was round, until he proved them wrong."

"I'll grant you that. But until you show me an extraterrestrial kidnapper, or a Star Trek transporter that actually works, I can't support your 'poof' theory. I teach science. I deal in hard facts. I examine the world as it is, not how some people would like it to be."

With that, there wasn't much left to say. I came to Miss Jeffries looking for answers, but left with even more questions.

"Thanks for your time, Miss Jeffries," I said.

"Not at all, Amy. You're always good for stimulating conversation. You'll make a great fiction writer someday."

Chapter 3

Graduation

To the sports-loving citizens of Shankstonville, our high school football field is sacred ground. Anyone not attending night games on Fridays, faced certain public ridicule on Saturdays. That's just the way it is.

Our outdoor stadium also hosted soccer matches and track meets, but on that bright afternoon, the chalk lines were used to align rows of folding chairs. A portable stage supported music stands, the American flag, and a student-built podium. The bleachers were filled with family and friends of the Senior Class gathered on the lawn. The students were decked out in matching black gowns. It was graduation day at Shankstonville High School.

I had volunteered to assist in handing out the diplomas. Among the honorees would be my night caller's daughter. I needed to speak with her, but not knowing her last name or what she looked like, there was no way to identify her. My on-stage duties would provide me an up-close look at each graduating student, and with a little luck, I would find the girl with the birthmark on her nose.

The proceedings began with the school band playing uplifting songs like "Climb Every Mountain" and "Walk On," concluding with a musical farewell selected by our teaching staff, "Hit The Road, Jack." Then came a long-winded speech by our principal, where he reminded us that the "path through life is forged by perseverance." If only he had conveyed that message to the students when classes were in session, we might have seen fewer dropouts.

After a few meaningless tributes and a benediction from the pastor of The Sins of Man church, the star of the show was introduced: the valedictorian. His name was Arthur Farthington, Jr. He delivered an inspiring speech about self-confidence and overcoming adversity. The program listed the title of his talk as *Make an Elephant Fly*. Besides his obvious reference to Dumbo, the flying elephant, his choice of words was interesting for two reasons:

First, it was well known that Arthur had a passion for aviation. His dad was an airline pilot, and urged him to pursue a career in aircraft design. He was already taking introductory college courses in Aerodynamics.

Second, we were shocked that he would mention an elephant. Arthur weighed well over 300 lbs. He had been teased mercilessly for his size all through high school. Then there was the unfortunate gym class incident. He had just consumed a large bowl of three-bean soup for lunch, and was doing sit-ups alongside his classmates. Suddenly . . . well, we all know what a release valve on a pressure cooker is for. He was thereafter known around campus as "Artie Farty", a nickname he would never live down. Yet, there he was, on stage in a graduation gown, looking like a house that had been tented for termite extermination.

With all the formalities out of the way, the band conductor lowered his baton to the downbeat of "Pomp and Circumstance." Students filed onto the stage as their names were called to receive their diplomas. Most accepted theirs in a dignified manner, while others chose to display a little more flair. Pumping your fist in the air while whooping to your buddies on the field was a common one. Some twirled their diplomas like those street corner sign spinners. The top prize, however, had to go to the boy who break-danced his way to the podium.

Then the name *Debra Fink* was called. She severely lacked that spark I had seen in the other seniors. With her head down, she shuffled quickly to the podium and grabbed her diploma, like stealing an apple off a fruit cart. She made a hasty exit, but not so hurried that I didn't see the small dot on her nose. I had found the mystery girl I was searching for!

With the students back in their seats, the principal offered his closing remarks. He then announce to the audience, "Ladies and gentlemen: Shankstonville High School's graduating class!"

The proud graduates stood up and cheered, as hundreds of black caps filled the sky, like a flock of crows flying off to roost.

I looked for Debbie Fink in the crowd, but I lost her in the sea of black. I was afraid that I had missed my only chance to talk to her, until I noticed a billowing black gown trotting out into the parking lot. I chased after the lone figure, that had stopped at a late model Honda Civic. Creeping up behind the car, I noticed a decal in the rear window displaying the initials *D.F.*

"Excuse me," I said. "Are you Debbie Fink?"

A hand quickly concealed her tear-stained face. "I don't want to talk right now, if you don't mind."

"Everyone's at the big reception in the gym," I said. "Aren't you going?"

"I told you I don't want to talk!" She reached to open the car door, but I held it shut with my hand.

"My name's Amy. I've come here to see you."

She peeked over the top of her fingertips. "Why do you want to see me? I don't even know you."

"I know your dad."

She angrily forced my hand away from the door, then climbed in and slammed it shut.

"Is he why you're so upset?" I asked.

Debbie rolled down the window and said sternly, "He didn't come, alright? My own father can't be bothered to see his own daughter graduate." She started the engine. "And you're a big, fat liar!"

"Wait!" I cried, as the car drove off. I cupped my hands around my mouth and shouted, "You're his little cherub!"

The break lights lit up as the car screeched to a halt. The engine was still running as I ran over to her. The distraught girl stared mournfully out the windshield and said softly, "I'm sorry I called you a liar."

Poor Debbie Fink. Her no-show dad had hurt her deeply, and I was only making things worse.

"You know what?" I said. "All this running has left my throat a little parched. Think I'll wet my whistle with some of that reception punch. Care to join me?"

Wiping away a tear, Debbie faced me. "I'd like that."

The crowd that had filled the football field now jammed the school gymnasium. Everywhere you looked were smiles and handshakes of congratulations. Girls shared hugs with weepy mothers. Boys endured hardy backslaps from proud fathers. A long refreshment table was laid out, offering coffee, cookies, punch, and a humongous cake with *Congratulations Grads!* spelled out in candy letters.

Debbie slipped into the girl's room to put her face back on, while I grabbed us each a Styrofoam cupful of punch.

We met up at a quiet table, far from the guitar-picking country band, playing selections from the Willie Nelson songbook. Sitting quietly, we sipped our punch. I wasn't sure how to begin our conversation. Debbie appeared equally uncomfortable. She gazed out at her fellow graduates, avoiding eye-contact with me.

To break the ice, I raised my cup. "Congratulations!" I said. We thumped our cups together to toast her academic achievement. Debbie's smile was far from genuine.

She circled her finger around the rim of her cup nervously, then said, "I don't mind telling you, but I feel a little awkward."

"Me, too," I said.

She looked hard at me, as if sizing me up. "So, you know my father."

It was a straightforward statement, but one I wasn't prepared to respond to. The fact was, I really didn't know her dad at all. I only knew why he missed her graduation: he drove himself over a cliff the night before.

I had to say something, but not *that!* Informing Debbie of her father's suicide attempt would break her heart. Telling her that he was a wanted terrorist wasn't going to brighten her day, either. I had sought her out to learn the identity of my mystery caller, not to be the bearer of bad news. I had to remember that.

"Your dad called me last night," I said.

"Oh?" Debbie's eyes narrowed with suspicion. "What did you say your name was?"

"Amy. Amy Dawson."

"Funny, my dad never mentioned you."

"We only met eight hours ago."

I didn't have to be a mind-reader to know what she was thinking. The contemptuous look on her face and her clenched fist said it all.

"It's all perfectly innocent," I assured her. "He dialed the wrong number and got me by mistake."

She wasn't convinced. "Really? What did you talk about?"

"You, for one thing."

"What about me?"

"He said he wished you hadn't hung up on him."

Debbie's face flushed as she fell back into her chair. It took her a moment to grasp that I knew the details of their private conversation. Then she took a deep breath and sat up. Reaching under her gown, she pulled out a whisky flask containing, I assumed, that intoxicating substance.

Looking warily around the room, she topped off her punch with it, and whispered, "I keep this for emergencies. Have some?"

"No thanks," I said.

"Guess you've figured out by now, my dad and I don't get along."

"You may not believe this, but he wanted to be here today. He had an awesome graduation present for you."

"You mean that ugly truck? I wouldn't be caught dead in that thing. Just shows how well he knows me."

"Why did you tell the police he had stolen it?"

"I was pissed! I know I shouldn't have done it. Guess I can't blame him for not showing up after what I did." She took a long swig of her special punch. "I hardly know my dad. He's always away on business."

She handed me his business card. "This is him."

Harley Fink
Investment Consultant

At last, my caller now had a name!

I showed Debbie my barbershop card. "Is this one of his clients?"

Debbie squinted as she held the card close to her face. "Ravi. Never heard of anyone with that name, or this salon. Maybe he's my dad's hairdresser."

"You think so?"

"Can't say for sure. Seems like he's always at the

barbershop. I suppose you have to look good in his line of work." She topped off her punch with more of her secret sauce and guzzled it down. "I shouldn't complain, though. Our best times together are always after he's seen his barber. He comes home a different person. Happy. Funny. He'll take me out to a movie, or a concert, or wherever I want."

Debbie's comment added a curious piece to the puzzle. For sure, sporting a handsome head of hair would improve anyone's self-esteem. For Harley Fink, however, it seemed to transform his personality. That burnt business card had more significance than I thought.

"Not to change the subject," said Debbie, "but is *he* with you?" She nodded toward a tall man leaning against the wall, alone, eating a slice of graduation cake from a paper plate.

"I've never seen him before," I said. "Why do you ask?"

"I noticed him at the ceremony, and again in the parking lot. Now he shows up here. I think he's following me."

The police were obviously on my tail, hoping that I would lead them to the felon who had slipped through their fingers.

"He's not following you," I said. "He's after me. He thinks I'm a terrorist."

We stared at each other stone-faced for a

moment, then burst out laughing. I swung around to get a second look at the man shadowing me, but he was gone. At least now I knew I was under surveillance. I was afraid that being seen with Debbie might put her in danger. But, without a positive ID on her dad, there was no way to link her to the crime.

I heard the sound of giggling, as two gowned girls skipped over to us. "Hey, Debbie!" said one of them. "We've been looking all over for you."

Debbie hid her empty flask under her gown and wobbled to her feet. "Amy, I'd like you to meet the two best friends a girl ever had." She stumbled over her chair attempting a group hug with them. "Can't get through life without friends."

The other girl rolled her eyes. "She's not usually like this," she told me. "Must be an emergency."

"It's been a trying day for her," I said. "Let her enjoy the rest of it."

Debbie reached out and shook my hand. "Have to leave you now, Amy. Me and my chums got some celebratin' to do. We just graduated high school, you know."

"Knock yourself out," I laughed. "You're halfway there anyway."

"Oh, and do me a favor. If my dad calls again, tell him I'm sorry . . . for everything."

"I'm sure he understands. No need to feel guilty."

She leaned into my ear, and with whisky on her

breath, whispered, "We're all guilty of something, aren't we?"

With Debbie gone, I finished my punch and left the table. A drum roll sounded from the stage, as all of the principal players in the day's festivities took their final bows—teachers, administrators, honor students.

But one key person was missing from the lineup: Arthur Farthington, Jr. I found him outside, tossing his cap and gown into the back of a white van. Painted on the side was *Boeing Aviation, Aerospace Division*. Artie Farty had shown such great promise as an aircraft engineer that the company recruited him right out of high school.

Dumbo would have been proud. The elephant had flown.

Chapter 4

The Barber Zone

*S**nipper Jim's*** was the newest and trendiest hair salon in Shankstonville. From Blowouts to Shags, it was the local one-stop shop for the latest in hair design. No more leaving town to get that Big City look.

Everyone knew its owner and hairstylist "Snipper" Jim from his zany TV commercials. In his signature pompadour and goatee, he was the quintessential late-night pitchman. He *cut* hair while *slashing* prices. "SAVE, SAVE, SAVE! on a SHAVE, SHAVE, SHAVE!" Every ad concluded with Jim spinning in a barber chair and promising, "No one leaves without looking fabulous!"

His storefront was impossible to miss, with its pink and purple color scheme and its owner's dashing smile on a rooftop billboard. Most days you could find Jim standing out front with a burning cigarette between his fingers. That's because his shop was usually empty. In spite of being an infomercial icon, he had mistakenly underestimated the demand for his services. Most of our rural townsfolk saw little value in parading around town in a sheik hairdo.

Jim's other mistake was that he did everything on the cheap. To save on rent, he set up shop in the old part of town, where no one shops anymore. The opening of Happy Fun Mart, our town's big-box superstore, had forced nearly every downtown retailer out of business. The streets were usually empty, as if a giant tsunami had sent the entire population scurrying for higher ground. Abandoned buildings stood like concrete ghosts in some apocalyptic movie. Faded signs left haunting reminders of the once thriving businesses: Jerry's Jewelers, Happy Day Greeting Cards, Carlyle's Cafeteria. Evidence of the merchant's last-ditch attempt to stay alive still hangs over the street: a torn banner proclaiming, *Downtown Has Everything!*

A few places managed to stay afloat, however, like the 24-hour Jiffy-Q convenience store. People still needed somewhere to buy diapers in the middle of the night. Charlie's Saloon also survived, providing folks a hideaway from such domestic chores. Then there was Snipper Jim's competition directly across the street from him: *Ravi's 2-Bit Solution* barbershop.

The shop's aging storefront was in desperate

need of a facelift. Its flaking wood siding showed signs of termite damage. The old spiraling barber pole had frozen in place decades earlier.

How the old shop managed to stay open was a favorite topic of local gossip. Some claimed that Ravi was selling services unrelated to hair care— *illicit* services, if you know what I mean. I'm not the kind to believe rumors, but the gossipmongers had pretty good evidence to support their suspicions. Finding a parked car out front was rare, but when you did, it was typically a stretch limo, a Rolls-Royce, or some other chauffeur-driven vehicle.

Such was the case as I pulled up behind a long, black Mercedes. I waited in my car to get a glimpse of who it belonged to. After a minute or two, the shop's door flew open. Out rushed two big men in dark suits. A third man then came out and was immediately hustled into the luxury car. The engine raced as the limo sped off in a cloud of exhaust fumes and dust.

I stepped out of my own version of vehicular opulence: my 1968 Volkswagen bug.

As usual, the streets were deserted. Wind whistled through the bare branches of dead trees. Except for two stray dogs growling over a discarded hamburger wrapper, I was completely alone.

At least I wouldn't have to worry about being spotted in the seedy neighborhood. That was before I noticed a puff of cigarette smoke rising across the street. Snipper Jim had been watching me from his salon. I smiled and gave him a wave. He raised his arm as if offering me a friendly welcome, but he was only taking another drag on his cigarette.

I crept cautiously toward the 2-Bit Solution, like I was in the shadow of a haunted house. Above the tarnished brass door handle was a hand-lettered sign that read,

BY APPOINTMENT ONLY
NO EXCEPTIONS!

I hadn't called ahead, but why would I do that? If you want to catch a thief in the act, you don't tell him you're on your way.

Jingle-ding-ding!

A small bell hanging above the front door announced my arrival. There was a distinct mustiness in the air, masked by the scent of baby powder. As expected, the shop's interior was as derelict as it was outside. Above me spun a squeaky, old ceiling fan. Under my feet was a scuffed checkered floor. The garish green walls had as much class as a gas station restroom. Though the shop looked destined for demolition, it also had an undeniable charm about it. It was like stepping into an *Andy Griffith Show* rerun. I could almost hear Floyd the barber snipping away at Barney's thinning hair.

Closing the door, I was standing in the waiting area. A glass display case separated customers from the barber's work space. Inside the case was a collection of novelty shaving mugs. Most were comical, like the one shaped like a toilet bowl. Others were printed with funny slogans, such as *Take it all off* and *I like you better with a beard.*

Beyond the showcase, a counter ran along one wall, filled with an assortment of scissors, combs, creams, lotions, and such. Then there was the barber chair—an antique if I ever saw one. The only thing missing from this setting was an old-time barber, with a handlebar mustache, in a striped shirt and bow tie.

"Hello?" I called out.

No reply. Perhaps the door bell hadn't rung loud enough, or Ravi was napping in a back room.

Then I heard the sound of rustling paper. I was so taken with the little shop that I hadn't noticed the gentleman seated in the corner. His face was hidden behind a newspaper. Only his salt-and-pepper hair was visible over the top. I quietly took a seat across the room.

There I waited.

It wasn't long before I started fidgeting from the boredom. The *squeak* of each turn of the ceiling fan wore on my nerves. A wall clock's *tick-tock* became a ping-pong match between my ears.

I impatiently drummed my fingers on the chair's

armrest.

"Ahem!" uttered the other customer.

"Sorry," I said. "I didn't mean to disturb you."

The bronze-skinned man turned the page of his newspaper with no further comment.

"Come here often?" I asked him. A pair of dark eyes glared at me over the headline. I had hoped to pass the time with a little light conversation, but I guess some people don't take kindly to small talk.

He resumed his reading, when I heard a low voice speak from behind the front page: "You make me . . ."

"Beg your pardon?" I said.

He turned another page. "You make me . . ."

I glanced around the room. "You're not talking to someone else, are you?"

Annoyed, the man flung his newspaper aside and stood up. His irritation was apparent as he marched toward me. I must have disturbed him more than I thought.

Looming over me, I noticed a comb tucked into the breast pocket of his white coat.

"Oh! You must be the barber," I said.

He wiped his thick mustache with the back of his hand. Then, surprisingly, his eyebrows went up. A broad grin crossed his lips. "You make me . . . *smile!*"

He grabbed hold of my hands, lifted me out of my chair, and began whirling me around like we were ballroom dancing.

"You make me smile!"

It all happened so fast that I didn't know how to react, but I followed his dance steps anyway. Oddly, I didn't feel threatened by him. I sensed more playfulness in his behavior than danger. And as I watched his grinning face, I smiled, too.

He sang:

"Yoooou maaaake meeee smiiiile!"

"Yoooou maaaake meeee smiiiile!"

Tripping over his feet, I said, "I'm afraid I'm not very good at this."

"Neither am I!" he blurted out in laughter.

Out of breath, the high-spirited barber waltzed me into the barber chair.

"What was all *that* about?" I asked him. "You take a happy pill this morning or something?"

"No need for that," he said, with a charming Middle-Eastern accent. "I'll take your delightful company over Prozac any day."

"You're Ravi, I take it."

He bowed. "Ravi Hakeem: here to fulfill your hairstyling wishes. And what, my sweet bird of youth, might your name be?"

"My name's—"

"No, don't! Let me guess. It's Aurora: the goddess of dawn, who sweeps across the morning sky to announce the new day."

"Nope."

"Iris: the rainbow goddess."

"Wrong again. It's Amy."

"Amy!" He clasped his hands together and gazed up toward the heavens, then paused. "I don't think there's a Greek goddess for you."

For sure, the barber showed all the craziness of someone who had escaped the loony bin, but I didn't care. I liked him.

Ravi pumped the barber chair pedal, bouncing me to the optimum haircutting height.

"I guess I should have made an appointment, huh?" I said.

Ravi waved his finger. "Tut-tut. Not another word. Now, what'll it be? Color, cut, and blow dry, or a full makeover?"

"Just a trim, please."

A quarter-turn of the barber chair and I was facing a large, round wall mirror.

"Ooh!" said Ravi. "I love this blue highlight in the back of your hair. How about a new color—say, green, or purple?"

"Don't even!" I warned him. "You want to ruin my image? That's my symbol of defiance."

Ravi rolled his eyes and sighed. "Just what we need: another rebellious teenager."

Of course, I hadn't come there for a haircut at all. Ravi was somehow connected to Harley Fink's disappearance, and this was the perfect setup for gathering information.

I watched Ravi standing behind me in the mirror, as he snipped the tips of my hair. "How is it that you're still in business?" I asked. "This whole block looks like a bombing range, and yet, here you are, a little single-chair shop."

"It's actually a *dual*-chair shop," he said. "I have a private parlor in back. Some of my customers are funny about being seen having their gray colored."

"You mean, like celebrities? That man I saw leaving here. Is he famous?"

"Not really. He just collects expensive cars."

"Any of your clients drive those huge trucks? You know, those big, black pickups that can crash through a brick wall and come out the other side without a scratch?"

I watched his reaction closely. "Not that I've seen," he replied.

He didn't so much as flinch at my description of Harley Fink's truck. Bringing those details into our conversation was probably not a smart move. If Ravi suspected that something fishy was going on, our little chat would be over before my split ends hit the floor.

"If you don't mind me asking," said Ravi, "what brings you to my shop, of all places?"

I was afraid of that. With my nosiness, I had carelessly given myself away. Now *I* was the one under suspicion.

I showed Ravi my barbershop business card. "I

found this laying on the ground, and thought, let's give him a try."

Ravi's eyes widened as he examined the card. "W-where did you find this?"

Ah-ha! There was a definite quiver in his voice. No doubt about it. Seeing that scorched calling card had him worried.

I was finally making some headway, when—

Jingle-ding-ding!

Through the front door walked a nice-looking young man. He was the athletic type, muscular, like he had just come from a workout. The display case blocked my full view of him, but from the waist up, he was a definite candidate for the firefighters calendar.

Without saying a word, he reached for a broom and began sweeping. His biceps bulged under the sleeves of his khaki t-shirt.

"Mornin', Alec," Ravi said to the man.

"Mornin', Dad," he muttered back, his eyes facing the floor.

"Has the daylight blinded you, son," said Ravi, "or have you forgotten how to act in the presence of a young lady?"

Alec's gaze remained on his feet, as he continued sweeping in silence. His broom bristles reached past the display case. Stepping beyond the barrier, I saw that he was wearing shorts. Then I gasped. His strong build was supported by only one leg! The other had been fitted with a prosthetic limb.

"This is Amy," Ravi said. "Say hello."

Alec tapped his broom on the floor to shake off the dust. Looking down, he said meekly, "Hello."

Then he lifted his head up to me. It was a quick glance, lasting no more than a second. His eyes were cold and lifeless. Suddenly, in that blink-of-an-eye moment, the young man's face filled with life. The faintest smile crossed his lips—a mere lift at the corners of his mouth.

Realizing that he had become the center of attention, Alec's eyes returned to the floor. "Ah . . ." he stammered. "I think I'll go out and sweep the sidewalk."

The little bell over the door nearly rattled off its hinge, as Alec dashed out the door with his broom.

Ravi's scissors had stopped snipping. His stunned expression reflected large in the mirror.

"Did you see that?" he said.

"See what?" I said, puzzled by his astonishment.

Ravi's lip quivered. "He smiled! Alec hasn't done that since coming home from the war."

Ravi's response needed no explanation. We've all seen the distressing images of traumatized war veterans—the retreat from society, the broken spirit, the amputated limbs. Like many small towns, Shankstonville had sent its boldest and bravest to face the brutality of modern warfare. Now, I was seeing its aftermath firsthand.

Ravi composed himself and went back to cutting my hair. "Sorry you didn't get a proper introduction," he said. "My son's having problems readjusting."

"His leg?"

"If only that was all. Do you know what PTSD is?"

"Sort of. I know it's a mental disorder. It causes soldiers to relive their wartime experiences in nightmares."

"That's not the half of it. A loud noise or a disturbing sight can bring on excruciating flash-backs. They abuse drugs. They drink themselves unconscious. Sometimes the emotional scars are so deep they become suicidal. Many vets never get over it." He wiped his teary eyes. "Alec has it. A terrible thing at only 26 years old."

The agony Ravi was suffering was hard to watch. My own tears fell imagining the horror Alec must be enduring. But I had tears enough for Ravi, too. Who is to say that a father's grief is any less painful?

"How's his mother taking it?" I said.

"She died before he was a year old. She'd be awfully proud of him, though. He's earned tons of medals for heroism."

Ravi calmly walked me over to the rinse basin for a shampoo, offering nothing more about his personal tragedy. A blow-dry and a few touch ups, and I stepped down off the old barber chair.

"What do I owe you?" I asked.

"Two bits," he said. "New customers get a special discount."

I handed him a quarter. "You're gonna go broke that way."

"Not at all. In fact, business is so brisk that I'm considering bringing on extra help. How would you like a job?"

"A job? Doing what?"

"Receptionist. It's easy. Take calls, make coffee, work the cash register. Consider it a summer position. What do you say?"

I had come to the 2-Bit Solution barbershop to find answers. So far, I had next to none. If Ravi couldn't help me, I thought, maybe *Alec* could. For whatever reason, he seemed to like me, but involving him in my adventure might be crossing the line. PTSD isn't an illness to be taken lightly. The suicide statistics resulting from it are staggering.

As for Ravi, it wasn't hard to see through his smoke screen. He needed a receptionist like he needed a fleet of ships. Alec's attraction toward me was apparently a breakthrough, and Ravi figured having me close by might help his recovery.

I was fine with that. But, I couldn't get too close to Alec. He was a good-looking guy, and all that, but he was ten years older than me, and getting involved with an older man wasn't on my to-do list.

Still, working for Ravi offered me a chance to unravel the mystery behind Harley Fink.

I turned to Ravi and reached out my hand to him.

"How does the day after tomorrow sound?"

Chapter 5

War Wounds

*H*ubert and I trusted each other implicitly. If he told me that sheep could fly, I believed him. If I said that a man vanished while driving his car over a cliff, he didn't question it. Hubert especially liked those kinds of fantastic stories. He was a natural born problem-solver, and loved exploring how the impossible might actually be probable.

He had his own method for developing theories. First, he used the intellectual approach. What physical evidence was there? What rational conclusions can be drawn? If there were no hard facts, he turned to his imagination. That was easy for Hubert. If his nose wasn't buried in a science textbook, it was deep in a comic book. He may have been a student of logic, but he was headmaster at the University of Comic-con.

After bringing Hubert up to speed on my search for Harley Fink, these were the theories he came up with:

On How He Evaded the Police

"This is a classic example of shape-shifting. Medieval folklore is full of tales where humans transform into animals—ravens, toads, rats. The police couldn't find Harley Fink because he changed physically. He turned himself into a toad and hopped out the car window."

On Disappearing

"Like Miss Jeffries says, things don't simply disappear, but they *can* change to another state. Leave an ice cube out on the counter and it melts. The solid object appears to have vanished, but it has merely assumed the form of water. Harley Fink didn't disappear, he melted! At this very moment, he may be a puddle, or hiding out in someone's backyard swimming pool."

On Ravi's Involvement

"Your barber is actually a wizard. He provided the catalyst that gave Harley Fink his magical powers. Harley might have drunk a magic potion. Ravi could have cast a spell on a piece of fruit. That's it! He provided the apple, and Harley bit into it."

On Alec

"No comment!"

Alec's attraction to me didn't sit well with Hubert. Ever since I rejected his offer to take me out, Hubert clams up at the thought of me with another boy.

"I knew this would happen," I said. "There's nothing going on between me and Alec."

"So you say. Then why did you take the barbershop job?"

"I told you. To get information."

"And what else?"

Hubert insisted he was only trying to save me some heartache, but I knew better. He was showing the jealous side of his personality. Of course, I knew exactly how he felt. I experienced that same emotion when he agreed to date Lydia, only I kept my feelings to myself. Hubert's protest was actually kind of flattering. It gave me a little buzz, even though you shouldn't gain pleasure from someone else's grief.

Hubert calmed down after I told him about Alec's battle with PTSD. He was familiar with the disorder, and the difficulties in overcoming it. He suggested that If I truly wanted to help Alec, that I learn more about his affliction—and Hubert knew just where to go for advice.

Leisure Dale Manor was a retiree's dream—big, airy, modern, with lots of activities for seniors. It was the perfect place to live out your golden years. The smell of fresh-cut flowers was everywhere. Its residents were well cared for and thoroughly content. The only bad apple of the bunch was Hubert's grandfather, Lester.

Hubert and I often stopped by the retirement home to lunch with him. Grandpa Lester was a strange old coot with a peculiar sense of humor, but you never heard anyone say a harsh word against him.

Our visit was more of a fact-finding mission than a get-together. Lester had been a Medical Corps officer in Vietnam, and had experience attending to soldiers with PTSD.

"Hello, again," said the young woman at the reception desk.

"How's my grandpa doing today?" asked Hubert.

"In rare form. So far this morning he pinched two nurses, and came to breakfast with a bed pan on his head." She picked up the house phone. "I'll let him know you're on your way up."

Lester's 2nd-floor apartment was modest in size, yet very comfortable. A large picture window overlooked a lush courtyard garden. It was warm and cozy, and except for smelling like sweaty socks, very homey.

Lester was pretty sharp for an old guy. He was

well read, and did crossword puzzles like a fanatic. He could name old song titles, quote speeches from classic movies, and knew every line of every episode of *The Honeymooners*. Remembering names, however, was not one of his strong suits.

"Grandpa!" said Hubert.

"Humphrey!" said Lester.

His mobility wasn't so good either, which meant spending most of his day in a wheelchair. He struggled to stand up to greet us.

I rushed over to him. "Easy, Les," I said. "We're heading down to lunch in a minute."

Lester gazed up at me through thick prescription glasses, studying me like a rare painting. "Who's this pretty young thing?" he asked Hubert. "Your new girlfriend?"

I settled Lester back into his chair. "We've met before," I said. "I'm Amy. You haven't forgotten me already, have you?"

"Balderdash!" he exclaimed. "I never forget a face, especially one as radiant as yours."

It was a kind remark, and I would have blushed from his compliment, but Hubert's grandpa was having fun with me, and we all knew it.

We wheeled Lester down the wide hallways, past delicate women in walkers, and frail men with oxygen hoses in their nostrils. In the elevator two elderly ladies, wearing purple outfits with matching red sun hats, rode with us to the ground floor.

"Hi, Gladys. Hello, Gertrude," Lester said. "You both know my grandson, Harold."

"Yes," said one of the ladies, "And who is he with today?"

"This is Amy, his mistress."

The old gals giggled at his sauciness. One leaned over to me and whispered, "He's in rare form."

We entered the brightly-colored dining room to an old showtune playing over the sound system.

"'Mad Dogs and Englishmen,'" said Hubert's grandpa, "Noel Coward, 1931."

Old friends offered their hellos to Lester as we crossed the dining room. Settling ourselves around his table, I scooted Lester in. "That far enough?" I asked.

"Yes, thank you," he said. "How would you like to be my permanent caregiver?"

"You don't want Amy," Hubert interjected. "She can't afford the time. She's too busy making trouble for the rest of us."

Lester pinched my cheek. "What? This delicate flower?"

Our server breezed passed our table. "Lunch will be out in a minute."

I unfolded Lester's linen napkin into his lap. "Mind if I pick your brain while we wait?"

"Not much to pick," he said, "but you can try if you want to."

"What can you tell me about PTSD?"

"*Shell Shock.* That's what they called it in the first world war. Then it was changed to *Battle Fatigue.* Now, it's *Post Traumatic Stress Disorder.* A so much more pleasant name, don't you think? But no matter how you spell it, it's a horrible, debilitating illness."

"Is there a cure?"

Lester glared at me as if I had said something to offend him. "No cure!" he yelled. The heads of the other luncheon guests turned toward us.

"Grandpa!" said Hubert.

"Sorry. It's one of those things you can't help but get pissed off about."

"I've read that PTSD is treatable," I said.

"Somewhat, with therapy and medication. Sadly, not everyone responds well to it. Some learn to live with the disorder, and go on to live fairly normal lives. Others aren't so lucky. Then there are the ones who can't live with it at all."

"Suicide?"

Lester bowed his head, his mind traveling to some distant land. "I saw it in Nam. It happened to a buddy I served with. He survived that horror in the jungle, only to take his own life when he got home."

I gently placed my hand over his. "I'm sorry for asking these questions, but I need your help. I know someone with PTSD. What can I do to help him?"

Lester raised his eyes up to meet mine. "More

than you think, Amy. There's a far better treatment than anything the VA can offer. Love and understanding are incredible healers. Your friend feels alone and detached. Reconnect him with the living. His heart has darkened. You can brighten it. Create happy memories to replace those he carried with him out of battle."

Lester rolled his steak knife over with the cutting edge facing up. "PTSD is like this knife. Your friend balances precariously on its razor-sharp edge. On one side is the light of fulfillment. On the other, a lifetime of torment. His aching feet are cut and bleeding. He desperately wants off of it. Eventually, he will fall. Guide him toward that light. Let him fall into your life-renewing arms."

I was moved by Lester's hopefulness, and fearful of it at the same time. What he was asking me to do sounded too much like a commitment. I only wanted to help Alec, not take on his burden. Success would be fantastic, but failure could be deadly. I didn't want that responsibility, but I couldn't just turn away from it, either.

"How do I begin?"

"That's easy . . . listen! The time will come when he's ready to talk about his experience. When he speaks, hear him, and watch a miracle unfold."

"Lunch is served!" announced our perky server. Hot plates were set before each of us, consisting of a hot turkey sandwich with gravy and all the fixings.

"Again?" complained Lester. "It's Thanksgiving every day around here." He was back to his old, ornery self.

Hubert, who had kept silent throughout this whole discussion, said, "There's one other way to deal with this PTSD thing: prevention. End the wars. Do that and you eliminate the problem."

"Harry's right!" insisted Lester. The level of his voice started to rise again. He slammed the palm of his hand on the table. "No more wars, goddamn it!"

"Calm down, Grandpa. I was just making an observation."

The fire had returned to Lester's eyes. "Don't you see? It's the perfect remedy. I can't end war, but you can! Your *generation* can. These pricks in Washington ain't gonna do shit about it. Get your people off their lazy asses and get busy. Get elected to something: congressman, senator, *president!*"

He pushed up on his wheelchair arm rests and wobbled to his feat.

Hubert steadied him. "Grandpa! Get a grip!"

Lester picked up a fork and banged it loudly on his water glass. "Ladies and gentlemen!" he yelled, over the murmuring guests. "Your attention, please! I have an important announcement to make. The wars are over!" He slapped Hubert's shoulder. "Allow me to present the future President of the United States of America: my grandson, Hector!"

Under the circumstances, you wouldn't expect a

roomful of elderly adults, who could barely walk without assistance, to respond with much enthusiasm. But thunderous applause immediately followed Lester's remarks. Everyone who was able to, stood up. Cheers echoed down the hallways of the Geriatric Wing.

"Speech!" demanded the crowd.

Lester leaned in to Hubert's flushed face. "Your country awaits your instructions, Mr. President. Give'em hell!"

The seniors quieted down, granting Hubert their full attention.

He stood up. "I think my grandfather spoke a little out of turn. I don't know anything about running a country."

I threw down my napkin and jumped to my feet, adding, "But he knows what's right and what's good. It's time that my peers take their place in history, and this young man is as qualified as anyone to lead us. Aren't you, Henry?"

Hubert's mouth hung open. "Well, I *was* manager of the sophomore volleyball team once."

The silverware on our table rattled from the ovation. The elated seniors would have carried Hubert on their shoulders if they could. Hubert beamed and flashed the peace sign. I smiled, too. For sure, this little gathering wasn't going to change the world, but I savored the hope that its message might one day be embraced beyond those walls.

Things had returned to normal at Leisure Dale Manor. The dining room was rearranged for that night's Bingo party. Old ladies gathered in the TV room to watch reruns of *The Golden Girls*.

Wheeling Lester back to his room, Hubert helped him into his recliner. "Great rally today, Hayward," said Lester. "Let's do it again tonight."

A nurse knocked on the half-open door. "I think you've had enough excitement for one day." She came in with a pillow and stuffed it behind Lester's head.

"Guess we'll be on our way," said Hubert.

I gave Lester a peck on the cheek. "It was nice seeing you again, Les. Thanks for all your help."

"Nice to see you, too, Amy. If you'll excuse me, now, I think I'll take a nap." Leaning back in his chair, he gazed out his garden window before closing his tired eyes. "You know, you two make quite a handsome couple."

"See you next time, grandpa," he said.

"Next time . . . Hubert."

Chapter 6

Customer Service

*E*veryone experiences a "wow" moment sometime in their lives. It might be when seeing the Grand Canyon for the first time. Its striking beauty and sheer size are breathtaking. Your first look at the ocean causes the same reaction. You feel so small and insignificant. Movies can sometimes wow you, too. I still *ooh* and *aah* when Dorothy steps out of her gray farmhouse into the Technicolor Land of Oz. I share Charlie Bucket's exhilaration as he enters Willie Wonka's world of pure imagination.

That was how I felt on my first work day at Ravi's barbershop. I pushed open the weather-beaten door and entered a feast for the eyes! Gone were the shabby countertops, the cracked display case, and the squeaky ceiling fan. In its place was an exquisite shop, rivaling the finest European salons. I checked outside to make sure I hadn't gone into the wrong building. No, the broken barber pole and flaking paint were still there. Remarkably, Ravi had remodeled the interior in a single day!

Construction crews worked round the clock. They laid pink marble tile where the old checkered floor had been. Wall paper in elegant patterns was pasted over the dreary walls. A beautiful trophy case displayed Ravi's shaving mug collection. The mahogany woodwork, sconce lighting, and the ornate rinse basin were first-class all the way. And the biggest improvement of all: a new barber chair! Its shiny chrome pedestal and black leather upholstery gave the room real style. The only things untouched were the jingling door bell and the big round mirror. If the spirit of Floyd the barber had ever resided there, he had surely been evicted.

In my excitement, I had completely overlooked the brand new reception desk, marking the center of my own little domain. Its curved shape and modern design perfectly complimented the updated waiting area. I checked out the desktop, expecting to find the tools essential to being an efficient receptionist: a Bluetooth headset, a computer, an electronic cash register. But all I found was an appointment book and a pencil. The drawers were just as barren. Nothing in them but a box of Kleenex.

Ravi was nowhere around, so I decided to get

back on the case and do a little detective work. The back room seemed like a good place to start.

Down the rear hallway, newly-lacquered oak doors ran along the back wall. The first one opened onto a deserted alley. The next revealed a utility closet. I inspected a stack of clean towels on a shelf, looking for remnants of foul play—like maybe blood stains. (Sherlock Holmes would have done the same thing.) Next was the private parlor that Ravi had talked about. It was a carbon copy of the front room.

My search had turned up nothing out of the ordinary, until I came to the final door. Alongside the frame was one of those keypad locks, like you see in high-security buildings. There was no way to enter the room without knowing the numeric code. I assumed it was Ravi's business office, but what could be so valuable inside that it needed a lock like that? Keeping office equipment and bookkeeping records safe is one thing, but this was way overkill. For the heck of it, I jiggled the door knob, but the door wouldn't open.

The only other thing in the hall was the staircase to Ravi's 2nd-floor apartment. It was then that Ravi came through the door at the top. Coming downstairs, he smiled at me from the bottom step, and said, "How do you like it?"

"It's amazing!" I said. "But, why are you doing this now? You didn't do it for me, did you?"

"Let's just say you inspired it. Think of it like cleaning the house before you have company over."

That sounded reasonable enough, but I knew there was more to it. He was removing any objections I might have to working there. Making me feel special meant that I'd be less likely to quit, and Alec could spend more time with me.

As to the poorly-equipped reception desk, Ravi explained that my duties were to take calls, jot down appointments, and most importantly, make the coffee. I really had no right to complain. For sure, the work wasn't very challenging, but it was a cushy job—and I was getting paid!

Ravi left me in charge while he prepped the parlor for the day. I was just making my first pot of coffee when a bright light caught the corner of my eye. The sun was bouncing off the windshield of a car pulling up to the shop. I raced to my desk and put on a welcoming smile.

To my surprise, the door flew wide open. A man rushed inside. Slamming the door behind him, he immediately closed all the window blinds, then nervously gazed out at the street between the slats.

You would expect someone that jittery to be in a prison uniform, but the man was smartly dressed in a pinstriped suit. He acted like he was being followed, or maybe he was hiding from the Law. Either way, he raced in so quickly that he didn't realized there was someone else in his hideout.

"Good morning, sir." I said.

He jumped, startled by the sound of my voice. "Who are *you?*"

"I'm Ravi's new assistant," I said. "Do you have an appointment?"

The frazzled man charged my desk like an angry bull. "Where's Ravi?" he shouted.

By then, Ravi had heard the commotion and poked his head into the room. "Hello, Senator Reed. Come on back. I'm all ready for you."

The man hurried past me, mumbling, "Thank God!"

I knew who Senator Reed was. He once awarded me a certificate of achievement in a public ceremony. He was running for re-election then. The local Press was there to cover the event—and what politician doesn't want free publicity? The thing I remember most was seeing the senator arrive in a government limousine, complete with a motorcycle escort.

I figured it was now okay to open the blinds and let the daylight back in. Out the window I saw the senator's car parked at the curb. It was a subcompact rental. Seeing Senator Reed around town without a limo was unusual, and you *never* saw him without his security guards.

The shop was now filled with that heavenly, fresh-roasted coffee aroma. My first customer's hastiness gave me no chance to offer him a cup. I considered taking one to him in the parlor. Then the phone rang.

Ravi had instructed me on just what to say. "Good morning. Ravi's 2-Bit Solution barbershop: home of the happy hairdresser." (I added that last part myself.) "How can I help you?"

There was silence on the other end. Then a woman's voice spoke: "Who is this?"

That seemed to be the question of the day.

"I'm in charge of scheduling hair appointments, ma'am," I said.

Another moment of silence. "Let me speak to Ravi."

"I'm sorry. He's with a customer. Can I help you?"

I heard a long sigh. "Alright. Put me down for Tuesday at three o'clock,"

I opened my appointment book and flipped through the pages. Strangely, every one was blank. Not a single entry had been made.

"Yes," I said. "Ravi can see you then. May I have your name, please?"

Another awkward pause. *"Lady Litigation.* Ravi knows who I am."

"Can I have your phone num—"

She abruptly hung up.

I started penciling in the information, when, wouldn't you know it? The pencil lead broke, and I didn't have a sharpener. I heard chuckling that I figured was intended for me, but it was coming from the hall. Standing in the doorway were Ravi and Senator Reed, sharing a hearty laugh. The frenzied customer was now as happy as a sailor on shore leave. Curiously, not ten minutes had passed since he entered the parlor.

From the front door the senator smiled at me, "You're doing a great job, kid," he said. Then he skipped out to his rental car and sped away, all the while whistling. Ravi, too, whistled merrily as he retreated back into the parlor.

This was just plain weird. What had caused such a dramatic change in the senator's attitude? I conjured up images of alien beings taking over human bodies. Then I recalled the local rumors— those suspicions of illegal activity. Rumor or not, something had put that light in the senator's face, and Ravi was supplying the spark.

No sooner had the senator left, than another customer came through the door. This time it was an attractive young woman. She turned her body to the wall the moment she came inside. And no wonder: she was crying.

"Are you alright, miss?" I asked.

She turned slowly. Her beautiful, young face was all puffy and red. "Is this the place?" she said softly.

"What place are you looking for?"

She opened her purse and placed Ravi's business card on my desk. "Am I in the right barbershop?"

The card was exactly like the one found at Harley Fink's crash site.

I didn't quite know what to say, except, "Do you have an appointment?"

The woman choked up again. I brought out the Kleenex box from my drawer.

Ravi appeared. "I'm the hairdresser," he said. "What can I do for you?"

The distraught woman looked up at him with tears streaming down her face. "Please, sir. You've got to help me. My husband doesn't know I'm here. My kids are at my mother's. I don't have much time."

I quickly poured out a cup of coffee. "This'll help chase those blues away," I said with a smile. Ravi waved me off as he tenderly walked her to the back room.

Like the customer before her, the woman came out a short time later, beaming with joy. Her glowing face was clean and bright as a sunflower. She glided past me like someone in the midst of a beautiful dream.

To say that this was a crazy morning wouldn't begin to describe it. Ravi's regular clientele was a bizarre mix of corporate executives, financial managers, media moguls, lawyers, lobbyists, and land owners. They all came into the shop anxious and depressed, and left with a song on their lips and a spring in their step.

Whatever was going on back in that parlor, one thing was certain: *no* one was getting a hair cut. Every head of hair that went in came out looking exactly the same. I should have suspected something was up when that bald-headed priest walked in.

On top of that, my mastery of the coffee machine was going unappreciated. Not one customer accepted my offer of a cup of joe.

It was nearing the lunch hour when one last limo drove up. The man who climbed out was dressed in street clothes, with his face hidden under a hoodie. He was younger than the others I had seen that morning, and I sensed something familiar about him. He was proceeded by a gorilla-sized bodyguard.

The big goon approached me. "Tell Ravi that *Megaboy* is here," he said. The use of code names was another custom I had gotten used to.

"Do you have an appointment?" I asked, knowing by that time it was a stupid question.

The imposing man looked at me like I was a lowly insect to be stepped on. "Tell . . . him!"

"Come on back!" called Ravi from the parlor. Megaboy—or whatever his real name was—walked past me.

"Do I know you from somewhere?" I asked him.

The young man pulled back his hood, revealing a propeller-topped beanie on his head. His face had been on posters all over school: Z Beanie Run!

As the pop star sauntered off, Ravi came out. "It's just about your lunchtime, Amy," he said. "Before you go, be a dear and walk down to the Jiffy-Q and grab me a large Jiffy Fizz Cola, will you?"

"Sure you wouldn't rather have a cup of coffee?" I said. "I just made a fresh pot."

"Customer's waiting," he said, then hurried off.

I walked out the door and noticed that Snipper Jim wasn't out in front of his shop as usual. Then I smelled something burning. Jim was standing behind me, his head in a cloud of cigarette smoke.

"Aren't you on the wrong side of the street?" I asked him.

Jim took a long drag on his cig. "How does he do it?"

"How does who do what?"

"You know who I mean. I see all those rich folks comin' in here, while I hardly get one customer all day. What's Ravi's secret?"

I fanned the smoke away from my face. "Why don't you ask him yourself?"

"Me and him ain't on speakin' terms. But I'll tell ya what. You find out what he's sellin' and I'll make it worth your while."

"I can tell you right now for free. He sells happiness. People come in sad, and they leave happy. Simple as that."

"That don't tell me how he's doin' it."

"It's a puzzle to me, too. But anyone who can spread a little joy in this miserable world doesn't need to explain himself. You should try it sometime." I walked off, leaving Snipper Jim to stew over what I had said.

But, he had *me* thinking, too. He was asking the same question I had been asking myself all morning. Did Ravi possess some special gift, or was he an undercover drug lord?

I returned to the shop, with a large self-serve cup in hand, to find the *Closed* sign turned toward the street. With the door unlocked, I walked in and found Alec sitting in the barber chair, playing a video game on a handheld device.

"Is your dad here?" I asked him.

"He says for you to take the afternoon off," he said, staring at his screen.

It was pretty obvious that Ravi had arranged for Alec and I to be alone.

"I brought Ravi the Jiffy Fizz Cola he asked for," I said.

"Pour it down the sink. Sugary drinks are bad for you."

I went to the rinse basin while keeping my eye on Alec, even though he hadn't once looked up at me. Ol' Lester had stressed the importance of being available, should Alec want to share his dark past with me. With his shy ways, Alec was a little hard to read, but this didn't seem like the right time.

"Should I lock up?" I said.

"I'll take care of it."

I caught Alec's face in the mirror as I crossed the room. His head was now tilted up, his eyes watching my every move. Then I heard him mumble, "Do you . . .?"

"Do I what?"

I thought for a moment that he might want to talk to me after all, but he went back to his game.

"Is there a good place to have lunch around here?" I asked.

"Nowhere you'd like."

"Where do *you* go?"

"Someplace little girls shouldn't be seen."

I may have only been a teenager, but I had been around enough to know when I was getting the brush off. Unfortunately for Alec, he hadn't yet learned that I don't like being treated that way.

"Show me!" I demanded.

"What?"

"Show me this place I'm supposed to hate, or are you too busy?"

"I'd rather not."

"Why? Are you worried that I might like it? Are you afraid of being wrong, then having to apologize to a boneheaded girl?"

Alec turned off his device and jammed it into his pocket. "Alright, little miss know-it-all! But don't say I didn't warn you."

As he stepped off the barber chair, his false leg twisted under him. I quickly moved in to help keep him from falling, but his hand instantly went up, warning me to stay away.

For the first time, I saw the conflict that raged within him. His disability was robbing him of his dignity. He was a model of strength and a proud soldier, and he didn't want me to see his weakness. I was sorry, now, that I had badgered him. That might have been a big mistake.

Chapter 7

The Afternoon Off

My little Volkswagen beetle wasn't designed for broad-shouldered men like Alec. He sat in the car's passenger seat, his knees jammed against the dashboard. He would have preferred to drive us both to lunch in his own car. He was fully licensed, but driving tended to put him on edge. One of his nagging battlefield memories involved driving an armored Humvee across hostile terrain, and his fear of being in command of a vehicle had yet to be overcome.

Aside from Alec giving me directions, our trip to his lunchtime hangout was relatively quiet. He examined my car's interior, running his fingers over the wood grain glove box and vinyl headliner. My '68 VW had been restored to its original condition, and then some. His roaming eyes led him to some junk I had tossed into the back seat. One was a *Save the Northern White Rhino* bumper sticker. Finding my Agatha Christie book, he placed it on his lap and thumbed through its pages. "Have you read *Murder on the Orient Express?*" he asked.

What a shock! I would never have pegged Alec as the literary type. "You read?" I asked him.

"I did in high school—voraciously."

"You can borrow that one, if you want."

"Nah. Don't read much anymore."

I had bookmarked a page with a three-fold brochure from Leisure Dale Manor. "Planning an early retirement?" he said.

"That belongs to Hubert."

"Is he an old man?"

"He's my age."

"Boyfriend?"

"Just friends."

It was only small talk, but at least we were communicating. His curiosity about Hubert and me was unexpected. Maybe this was his way of permitting me to ask him more personal questions.

"You got a girlfriend?" I asked.

Alec flipped through the pages of the book, pretending not to hear my question. It was his way of telling me that delving into his personal life was a boundary not to be crossed.

While stopped at a red light, Alec leaned forward, staring at something out the windshield. "Pull over after we get through this intersection," he said.

On the far corner stood a haggard, middle-aged

man in military fatigues, holding up a cardboard sign that read *Homeless Vet. Please Help!*

Alec rolled down his window as I pulled up to the curb. The homeless man's skin was blackened from overexposure to the elements, and smelled like he hadn't bathed in months. Alec handed him a twenty-dollar bill. "Hang in there, buddy," he said.

The man smiled, showing his stained and missing teeth. "God bless you, sir!"

Alec saluted him before we continued on.

"I know you meant well," I said, "but how do you know what that man's going to do with that money? For all you know, that twenty will go to buy drugs."

"You could be right," said Alec. "I may have just been scammed, but sometimes you gotta take a chance on people."

I admired Alec's steadfast trust in his fellow man. It showed the goodwill in him. But, he didn't look overly thrilled in what he had just done. He didn't radiate that warm and fuzzy glow you're supposed to have. He seemed unsettled, as if he had seen *himself* on that street corner.

We rumbled over some railroad tracks where no train had traveled in years. On the other side was a rundown, old shack. "There!" said Alec, pointing to the public eyesore. It was a derelict beer joint—a perfect meeting place for bikers and boozers, but definitely not for me. In the window, above the flickering neon beer ads, hung a sign that read *Duke's Place.*

"*That's* where we're going?" I said.

"I told you you wouldn't like it."

He was right. I didn't. But confessing that would be admitting defeat. I had challenged Alec that any greasy spoon he chose, no matter how grungy, would be good enough for me, too. Now I had to prove it.

"Looks fine to me," I said, praying it wasn't so disgusting on the inside.

That nauseating smell of stale beer hit me the moment I walked through the door. The dark saloon looked exactly as I had imagined, from the moose head above the bar to the crushed peanut shells under my feet. The brawny men hunched over the bar turned and looked at me, like I was a pound of meat tossed into a lion's cage.

"Sit anywhere's y'all want," called out the husky-voiced bartender. He immediately spotted me as a minor. "Hey! She can't be here."

"It's cool, Duke," replied Alec. "How about a brew for me and a couple of lunch menus?" Sitting down at a booth, Alec smirked at me across the table. "Don't worry. I won't tell Hubert."

The heavyset barman waddled over with a bottle of Jiffy Beer and two menus, each one covered with grease stains. Mine was too gross to even pick up.

"I'm really not very hungry," I said.

"You hate it here," said Alec. "Admit it!"

"Actually, I kind of like it. It has . . . character."

I wished he would stop ragging on me about the stinky bar. I wanted to move on to something we could both relate to. But that wouldn't be easy. I knew nothing of Alec's interests, except for his attraction to books.

"I'm curious," I said. "What kind of books do you like? Have you read any of the classics?"

Alec twisted off his beer bottle cap. "Some."

"Really? What's your favorite?"

He leaned back, raised up his fake leg, then slammed it down on the tabletop. *"Moby Dick,"* he said. "Call me Captain Ahab."

"What did you do that for?"

"So you can get a better look at it. You've been staring at my leg ever since we met."

"That's not true."

"The hell! You look at it and wonder things like: How does he put his pants on in the morning? How does he shop for shoes? How does he go to the can on one leg?"

Alec's combative side was showing itself again. He was trying my patience, but I remained courteous.

"Why shouldn't I be curious?" I said. "It's a marvel of medical science. It helps people get back to normal."

Returning his metallic foot to the floor, he pulled

on a silver neck chain hanging down his shirt. Attached to it was a medallion, engraved with an image of a runner holding a flaming torch.

"See this?" he said. "Silver Medal: World Championship Finals, 800-meter Dash. You know how hard I worked to earn this? How many years I trained? Now, tell me about getting back to normal."

In my effort to boost Alec's self-esteem, I had tapped into that dark place I was trying to draw him out of. Staying positive was turning into a real chore.

"Have you considered the Paralympics?" I said.

"Don't you get it? I was an Olympic hopeful. Competing against the best in the world was my dream. I guess that's too much for a pinheaded teenager to comprehend."

"I know it's a setback. But you can't wall yourself off from the world because of it."

"You're just full of clever answers, aren't you? Well, let me ask *you* a few questions. Have you ever gone to a high school dance?"

"Yes." (I hadn't.)

"Ever thrown a pajama party."

"Yes." (I hadn't done that, either.)

"Ever teased a boy you like, just to get his attention?"

"Yes." (Another lie.)

"When's the last time you went on a date?"

His cockiness was really starting to annoy me. "What's your point?"

"You avoid human contact as much as I do. You connect better with rhinos than you do with people. You'd rather curl up with a book than a warm body."

Now I was really steamed!

"You're crazy!" I shouted.

"You're a hypocrite!" he fired back.

"You're a quitter!"

"You're a loser!"

Beer splashed onto the table as I batted the bottle away from his lips. "You're one to criticize. You've got no commitments. You've got no responsibilities. You hide out here like a mole, then use that damn leg as your excuse. People tell me, 'listen to him. Be sympathetic.' Well, that's what I've been doing, and now I'm asking myself, why bother? I should have never come with you to this dump. I hate it! I'm going back to the shop. You can *walk* back on your peg leg, for all I care."

I stood up to leave, mad as I've ever been, when Alec grabbed my arm and pulled me back into the booth.

"Thank you, Amy," he said calmly. "That's the first honest thing you've said to me."

The bartender shouted, "Pipe down over there, or I'm tossin' y'all out on your butts. Get it?"

"Got it," replied Alec, with that little smile I saw

that first day in the barbershop.

Giving our egos a rest, Alec and I engaged in a frank and cordial conversation. He talked for an hour—describing his combat victories, his defeats, and the explosion, from which he alone would survive. He didn't hold back his feelings, either, confessing the terror he felt on that traumatic day. He recounted the agony of his painful recovery, and the frustration from months of physical therapy. At times his mood swayed from resentment, to gratefulness, to bittersweet. But there was no arguing between us, no exchange of anger. I was careful not to press him for any details he wasn't comfortable sharing with me.

And while I listened, I watched in amazement as the weight of the world lifted from his shoulders, as if by angels. By the time he finished, he had not only earned my respect, but my heart, too. I was overcome with a peculiar closeness to him I had never felt before.

It was time to leave Duke's Place. Sliding to the edge of his bench seat, Alec caught his artificial limb on the table leg. He yanked on it with both hands, grunting like an animal with its foot in a trap. Freeing himself, I offered my hand to help him to his feet. This time he took it. Feeling his firm grip was like the two of us had merged into one.

As we walked out to the gravel parking lot, I was surprised to here Alec say, "I'll drive." I gave him a puzzled look. "I can do it," he said. "Really."

Alec had avoided any driving since his return from the war. I figured this was his way of proving his newfound confidence to me. Having mastered military vehicles, he was certainly capable of handling my little car. What worried me was the stick shift. He would have to shift gears using a clutch, and with no feeling in his left foot, how could he even find the pedal?

But this wasn't about his driving skills. He was testing my trust in his judgment. Or as Alec had so plainly put it, "Sometimes you gotta take a chance on people."

I handed him my car keys.

Alec drove us out into the street like an expert, observing all the traffic laws. He maintained a safe and sound speed, like an old spinster on her way to church.

"How am I doing?" he asked.

"Perfect," I said. "What made you decide to take up driving again?"

"Look behind us."

I glanced over my shoulder out the back window. "Yeah? So what?"

"See that red SUV two cars back? It passed the shop several times today. The same one followed you back from the Jiffy-Q, and it was just parked at Duke's Place." Alec shot me a suspicious look. "Is there something you're not telling me?"

Was there ever! I hadn't said a word about being under surveillance by the feds, who were surely behind us. I hadn't confessed that my whole reason for coming to the shop was to finagle information about Harley Fink. Confessing that to Alec would be risky. He might look at it as a betrayal of his trust, but I had to take that chance. He had just poured his heart out to me, and I felt that I had to level with him.

"The cops are following me," I said.

"For what? Are you a criminal?"

"*I'm* not, but they're hoping that I can lead them to one."

"And, can you?"

"No. I don't even know where he is."

Alec pondered my answers for a moment, then commanded, "Hang on!"

He downshifted into second gear, floored the gas pedal, then made a hard left just ahead of the oncoming cars. With the red SUV stuck in traffic behind us, we sped off toward open farm country.

Before long, we were whizzing past grazing sheep and fields dotted with hay bales. Our pursuers should have been miles away, but they somehow managed to catch up to us.

"Do you have to drive so fast?" I asked Alec. "It's not like they're shooting at us."

"The sure way to avoid casualties is to stay out of range, sir!" He sounded like a military combat commander. That worried me. Subjecting war veterans to battle-like situations can trigger flashbacks. But, Alec showed no signs of freaking out—rather, he seemed to be enjoying it all.

Up ahead was *Pa Parker's Pumpkin Patch*. Each year it hosted a seasonal festival, where locals came to mingle, feast on candy corn, and judge pumpkin pie-eating contests. With the autumn harvest still months away, the farm was an empty flatland.

At the entrance stood a massive walk-thru pumpkin—a throwback to those bizarre roadside attractions of the 1950s.

"How wide do you suppose that entryway is?" asked Alec.

"Five feet, if even that."

"Wide enough for us."

Alec raced toward the concrete pumpkin, and with only inches to spare, passed through its pedestrian entrance. The oversized SUV skidded to a halt behind us. We had escaped the claws of the cat by ducking into a mouse hole.

The chase was over, but Alec couldn't resist tormenting our opponents—parading back and forth past the narrow entrance, beeping his horn.

"You know they'll just go back to the shop," I said. "This didn't really accomplish anything."

"I know that," said Alec. "This game is rigged in their favor. But today, *we* won!"

Alec pulled up to the barbershop, turned off the

engine, and set the hand break.

"Well, that was quite an adventure," I said. "Thanks for the joy ride."

Alec didn't respond, not even offering so much as a "you're welcome." He just stared out the windshield, quiet. There was an uneasiness about him. I thought perhaps he had more to confide in me, but I quickly learned that talking wasn't on his mind.

I unbuckled my seat belt and reached for the door handle when I felt his hand on my knee. I froze. His touch set my whole body trembling. I knew immediately what was happening. Alec and I had shared a profound, personal connection. Together we had broken through his emotional barriers, but his physical needs remained unsatisfied, and I wasn't about to go there.

I slowly turned to face Alec. Still staring blindly out into space, I watched his shoulders rise and fall from his heavy breathing. Sweat beaded on his brow as he stroked my leg seductively. News stories of young girls being assaulted in broad daylight entered my mind. Here I was, alone with a man strong enough to overpower me, on an abandoned street. My racing heart felt like it was going to pound right out of my chest. He was the mighty jungle cat, and I was the frightened prey.

I reached for the ignition key, but Alec covered it with his hand. I should have bolted from the car right then, but I didn't want to leave him this way. I thought maybe we could talk this out. But I instead batted his hand away, yanked the car key from the ignition, and flew out of the car.

I stood with my back to the barbershop wall, shivering. In the car Alec was slumped over, his forehead against the steering wheel. I heard the muffled sounds of him wailing in agony. He was having a complete breakdown right in front of me, and there was nothing I could do to help him.

I screwed up. I was ignorant of the complexity of Alec's disorder—that it wasn't something you can reverse in a single afternoon. If only I had known how much more painful the wounded heart is, over the wounds of the flesh.

Finally, the car door opened. Out stepped Alec, calmly and quietly. His face was drained of all feeling. His reddened eyes didn't once look my way, as he unlocked the shop door and went inside.

Heaving a sigh of relief, I got back in the car. I sat there a moment, wondering what I should do now. I was supposed to return to the shop the next morning. What was I going to tell Ravi? Should I even attempt to see Alec again? Hopefully, a night's rest would lead to a promising solution.

I started the engine, when a shiny object caught my eye. Lying on the passenger's seat was a broken neck chain—and Alec's treasured medallion.

Chapter 8

The 2-Bit Solution

I arrived at the barbershop bright and early, way before opening. The night had cleared my head, allowing me to sort out the mishaps of the day before. I had prepared a speech to give to Alec, along with a pocketful of apologies. I wanted to show my regret for us getting off on the wrong *foot*—well, I wouldn't use those words exactly, but something to that effect. I had a speech for Ravi, too, suggesting that we share equally in furthering Alec's recovery.

I was chipper and ready to start the new day. My self-confidence wasn't the only thing I brought to work. My little dog Scraps came with me. A crew of painters were descending on our house that day, and my dad wanted to prevent any lawsuits resulting from a mean dog that bites. Of course, that same problem could arise at the shop, but I didn't see that happening. Scraps spent his days sleeping soundly in his doggie bed, and was perfectly harmless, so long as you didn't disturb him.

Ravi didn't see me come in to the shop. Standing at the round wall mirror, he gazed deeply into it. He wasn't looking at himself, but examining the reflection of the room behind him, as if searching for something. I hoped that this wasn't somehow tied to Alec and me, but the worried look on his face suggested otherwise. Something told me there would be no singing in the shop today.

"Mornin' Ravi," I said.

The surprised barber saw me, then turned back to the mirror, scraping on it with his fingernail.

"Anything wrong?" I asked.

"No, no," he said unconvincingly. "Just scraping the specs off this mirror."

Scraps barked at him from his pet carrier as I walked by, but Ravi didn't give it a second thought. He didn't even question me dragging my box of doggie supplies down the hallway.

I plopped Scraps' bed onto the floor, and by the time I finished filling his water bowl, he was already fast asleep. Good boy!

Ravi was now standing by the barber chair, holding a black cape out to his side like a Spanish matador. "Your hair looks a little frizzy," he said. "Hop up on the chair and I'll trim it up before we open."

I checked myself out in the mirror. "It looks fine to me."

"Now, Amy, who's the expert here?"

I climbed up onto the chair. Ravi seemed to be his old self again. He hummed while draping the cape over my shoulders. But as he ran his comb through my hair, I felt his hand trembling. Now I *knew* something was wrong.

"You closed early yesterday," I said.

"It was such a lovely afternoon," said Ravi. "How was your time off?"

I didn't know how much Alec had told him about us, if indeed he had said anything at all. Ravi might have been fishing for my version of what happened. I should have launched into a candid conversation with him right then, but I took the coward's way out. "Fine," I said.

The mirror reflected Ravi's sadness returning.

"Expecting a busy day today?" I asked.

His thoughts had drifted elsewhere. "What?"

"Today's appointments."

"Appointments?"

It was time to end this verbal Ping Pong match. "Where's Alec?"

His mournful eyes met mine in the mirror. "I'm sorry to tell you this, Amy. A terrible thing has happened. Alec is in the hospital."

I abruptly sat up. "What is it? Is he okay?"

Ravi settled me back into the chair. "It was late

last night. I called to Alec in his room. He didn't answer. Then I knocked on his door. Again, nothing. When I saw that the door was locked, I broke it down. I found him laying on his bed, unconscious. On the floor was an empty bottle of prescription painkillers. He had taken the whole bottle, Amy, the *whole* bottle!"

I bit down on my lip to keep from crying. "And?"

"Doctors say he'll be okay, thank God."

I was short of breath and numb down to my toes. The PTSD demons had mercilessly attacked Alec in the night, and I was the one who set them loose. I was so sure that I could help him, but like rescuing a drowning man without knowing how to swim, my ignorance nearly cost Alec his life.

"I did this to him!" I said. "It was me!"

"No, Amy. It was his illness."

"You're wrong. It's my fault."

"Please, don't blame yourself."

"Listen to me! Alec and I had a long talk yesterday—a *good* talk. He opened up to me about everything. I helped relieve him of his grief, but I couldn't relieve his loneliness. I hurt him, Ravi. I hurt him bad!"

Ravi stepped back and took a long look at me. "I understand," he said. "Let's wash your hair."

My lip was still quivering as he leaned my head back into the basin.

"I'm such a stupid ass," I said.

"Shh! Try to relax."

The warmth of the water flowing through my hair was calming. I was breathing easier. Ravi's gentle touch on my scalp brought on that sleepy feeling. I had just started to closed my eyes, when the water suddenly turned scorching hot!

I leaped out of the chair and dashed across the room. "What the hell are you doing?" I yelled. But Ravi ignored me, as if he hadn't heard a word I said. He remained hunched over the sink, the soapy water splashing over the sides. Then I realized that someone else was in my seat. However impossible that was, I moved closer to have a look.

The other person in the chair was . . . *me!*

This had to be a dream. I had fallen asleep, and my twisted imagination was taking over.

I heard a crackling noise above my head. Looking up, sparks were flying from the light fixtures. Out the window, the daylight had turned to night. A howling wind rattled the front door like a massive storm was approaching. It was a little frightening, but I kept telling myself, dreams can't hurt you, even one as real as this.

Feeling water between my toes, I looked at the floor. My dripping wet hair was forming a puddle under me. "Hey Ravi," I said, "Where's the mop? Cleanup on aisle five."

Looking down again, the water had risen over my ankles, and was rapidly filling the room like a dam had just burst.

The wind outside now whipped around at hurricane strength. Lightening flashed behind the window blinds.

I tapped Ravi on the shoulder. "How long is this dream gonna last?" I asked. He turned around, but it wasn't his face I saw. It was Alec's! This didn't surprise me. Dreams are always unpredictable, even more so when you're under emotional stress.

"What are you doing here?" I shouted, over the roaring thunder. "You're in the hospital."

"You sure about that?" he yelled back. "Does this look like a hospital to you?"

Suddenly, the lights went out. The violent wind blew open the front door. Water rushed in like a raging river. Now up to my knees in floodwater, I struggled to steady myself against the strong current.

Through the open door floated a rubber inner tube. Lying in it was Alec, happily splashing around like a kid at a water park—and he had *two* good legs!

"It's almost over!" he hollered, as he sailed past me.

A loud crash, and the shop windows shattered into little pieces. I closed my eyes and screamed, while shielding myself from the flying glass.

Finally, the storm passed. It was quiet. I heard the distant calling of song birds. My hair was now floating gently on a tropical breeze: the warm air from Ravi's blow dryer.

Opening my eyes, I was sitting comfortably in the barber chair. The morning light streamed in through the unbroken windows, and the floor was bone dry.

With a reassuring grin, Ravi asked, "How do you feel?"

"I just had the weirdest dream," I said.

He turned off his hair drier. "It seems that way sometimes."

"What does?"

His hesitation to answer worried me. "What did you do to me?" I demanded. "Why did you scald me with that hot water?"

"It has a burning effect when you're not use to it."

"Used to *what?*"

Ravi went to the shelf above the rinse basin and held up a shampoo bottle. Its handwritten label read *Guilt Remover*. "I shampooed your hair with this. It washes away guilt."

"You can't be serious. That's not possible."

"But, it *is!* I created it so that people wouldn't have to live with their guilt. Think of it as a kind of emotional reset button. Plus, it has a lovely bouquet, wouldn't you agree?"

Ravi was talking nonsense, but one thing was true: The guilt I suffered over Alec's attempted suicide was gone. In its place was a conviction that I had done all I could—that no one person should accept all the blame.

"Okay," I said. "Let's assume your shampoo does what you're telling me. Why invent it?"

"At some time in our lives, we've all done or said something we later regretted. Not everyone handles guilt the same way. Some simply ignore it. Others try to redeem themselves by making amends. Then there are those who find living with it unbearable. Those are the ones I try to help. You took on the blame for Alec's attempt to take his own life. That's a terrible burden for anyone to carry. You needed the Guilt Remover if anyone did."

So explains the parade of sorrowful customers. After committing some deplorable act, they come to Ravi seeking relief from their guilt. No wonder everyone left the shop so happy.

Ravi flung off my barber cape and lowered the chair. "Let me show you something."

He led me to the door with the digital lock. Entering the security code, it opened into another hallway. On the walls hung framed certificates—not from barber colleges, but famed universities, each recognizing Ravi for his achievements in scientific research. Among his other accolades were degrees in Chemistry, Biophysics, and Pharmacology. All were inscribed with Ravi's name in bold letters.

"You haven't always been a barber, have you?" I said.

"Let's just say it's not my calling." He opened the door at the end of the hall. "This is my *real* vocation."

Switching on the light, inside was a huge science laboratory. It resembled those you see in TV medical dramas, filled with lab equipment and scientific instruments. Odd-shaped flasks and glass beakers were filled with colorful liquids. Cabinet shelves held bottles of chemical compounds with long names I couldn't begin to pronounce. Among the hi-tech instruments were super-sensitive microscopes, scales that measured weight in micrograms, and those contraptions that spin test tubes like a high-speed carnival ride.

"I'm impressed," I said, "But I'm confused. If your discovery is such a scientific breakthrough, why put it in shampoo? Wouldn't it be easier to just give someone a pill?"

"A pill wouldn't be nearly as effective. Think about it. The hair on your head is just inches away from your brain. My formula penetrates the skull, and who else gets that close to your noodle but a brain surgeon or a hairdresser?"

There was a kind of madness to everything I was hearing. A shampoo that changes your personality was like something out of a Frankenstein novel. But Ravi had clearly done his homework, and his lab definitely wasn't a place where you'd find a mad scientist.

"I know it's none of my business," I said, "but, what's your shampoo's active ingredient?"

Ravi pointed to a large black and white photograph on the wall. It showed him standing on the banks of a muddy lake, surrounded by jungle foliage. Posing with him were members of a primitive tribe. Bare-breasted women carried babies on their hips. Bashful children poked their heads around bamboo trees. Naked men concealed their privates behind large leaves.

But a happier group photo you never saw. There were smiles all around—including Ravi, wearing an explorer outfit, complete with pith helmet.

"That's me in the Brazilian rainforest," he explained. "I joined an expedition seeking to learn about these remote people, known as the Wickagua tribe. Unlike the savagery of some primitive people, their whole culture was based on kindness. There were no words for *war* or *hate* in their language."

Ravi pointed out one native in particular, wearing the biggest grin of all. "When we first arrived, his hands were bound behind his back. Two husky men led him into this lake in full view of the tribe. The man struggled desperately to free himself, screaming like he was walking the last mile to the electric chair. Waist-deep in water, a tribesman dipped his head back into the lake. When he came back up for air, he was laughing uncontrollably, like he had just inherited a million dollars. The cheering tribe could be heard for miles."

"Something in the water, am I right?" I said.

"Exactly! But we didn't know what. The tribal council permitted us to bring a gallon of it back home for testing. Being the only biochemist on the trip, I was allowed to conduct my own studies. After years of experimentation, I was able to extract the water's miraculous properties."

"And so, the Guilt Remover."

"Yes, but that's only the beginning!"

Ravi keyed open a secure metal cabinet. Inside were more shampoo bottles with funny-sounding names, each with its own mind-altering capabilities:

The *Grief Reliever* eliminated sorrow. Anyone grieving the loss of a loved one can move on, free from heartache.

The *Hate Slayer* removed bigotry. Tolerance is restored in people harboring racial, religious, or other prejudices.

The *Temper Tweaker* eradicated aggression. Violent criminals released back into society become peaceful citizens.

"Very cool," I said, "but how can you afford to do this? You're a barber."

"You'd be surprised what people are willing to spend for my services. What do you think paid for this laboratory?"

Our conversation was abruptly interrupted by the sound of barking. Scraps was awake! Scampering down the hallway, he invaded the laboratory, yelping his mean little head off. I snatched him up into my arms.

Uncapping a bottle of Temper Tweaker, Ravi poured a small amount into the palm of his hand.

"What are you going to do?" I asked.

Ravi worked the solution into the fur on Scraps' head.

"Don't hurt him!" I cried. "You do, and I'll report you to the ASPC—"

All of a sudden, the barking stopped. I felt a wet tongue on my hand. Scraps was licking me! For the first time since rescuing him, I was able to pet my dog without fear of losing a finger.

"You won't have any problem with that mutt again," said Ravi. "He'll be a gentle lap dog from now on."

"This is incredible! The whole world should know about this."

"That's the whole idea. Independent studies have already declared my shampoos safe and effective. Medical journals will soon be featuring my discoveries. All that's left is FDA approval, and they're looking at samples as we speak."

Returning his shampoo to the cabinet, there were only a dozen or so more bottles. "I hope that isn't all you have," I said. "Satisfying worldwide demand is going to take a little more than that."

Ravi led me out into the back alley to a huge metal container. He opened a padlock and swung the solid doors open. Inside was a slew of 50-gallon drums, each one marked Guilt Remover.

"All this from one gallon of jungle water?" I said.

"A tiny amount, mixed with Hyaluronic Acid and alcohol, then diluted with tap water really stretches the soup."

"That leaves just one final question: Why are you showing me all this?"

"I have one more shampoo that I'm still developing, and I'm going to need your help testing it."

"Why? What does *it* do?"

"Cures PTSD."

Chapter 9

Mirror, Mirror

No one spent more time at the public library than Hubert did. If he couldn't find what he needed there, he scoured the shelves of used book stores. People have this delusion that everything we need to know can be found online. Hubert knew better. He dove into bookshelves like a pirate digging for buried treasure, and never failed to come up with a gem.

With his superior research skills, I recruited Hubert to help me learn more about the Wickagua tribe. I had already Googled those primitive people and found very little information. My Wiki searches produced even less. But while I was clicking links, Hubert had uncovered a goldmine that no one knew about, and wanted to show it to me in person.

With eyes wide with excitement, Hubert entered my room with a book under his arm. It was a musty old thing, with worm-eaten pages and a binding that would crumble in your hands if you weren't careful. Published in 1912, it was written by renowned South American explorer Arthur Gimbal, titled *Atonement in the Jungle*.

"Where did you find this?" I asked Hubert.

"At a flea market," he said. "I got a lead on a guy selling antique tribal masks, and this was among them. There's a whole chapter on the Wickaqua and their customs. Here's what I learned."

Hubert whipped out his notes.

"First of all, the name Wickagua literally means, 'to bathe the wicked.' The author writes about what he calls 'a baptism-like ritual'—the same ceremony Ravi observed. But, messing with people's minds wasn't the only supernatural power these guys were playing with."

Hubert cracked open his book. I nearly fell over from the smell of its moldy pages. An old photo showed the superstitious people kneeling on the ground in prayer. But, the object of their worship wasn't a golden calf. They were bowing to a mirror—a big, *round* mirror!

"I've seen that!" I said, excited. "It's the mirror in Ravi's barbershop."

Hubert pulled the book away from me. He didn't like being interrupted, especially when showing off his brilliance. "If you don't mind, may I continue?"

"Sorry."

"European colonization of the rainforest was underway about this time. Gimbal figured that the mirror must have fallen off a river boat, floated downstream, and later found washed ashore by the tribe. The primitive people had never seen a mirror before, and didn't know what to make of it."

"Let me guess," I said. "And seeing themselves in the reflection was a kind of miracle. So, they bowed down to the mirror like it was a god. Am I right?"

"Ahem!"

"Sorry."

"Yes, they were baffled by its reflectivity, but they prayed to the mirror for a different reason. They claimed they could communicate with the dead through it. Not only that, the dearly departed could climb out of it and rejoin the living. Gimbal claims to have actually seen it happen."

This was where I drew the line. The idea of psychedelic lake water was pretty hard to believe, but at least there was chemical science to support it. Seeing dead people in mirrors was going over the top. Maybe in 1912 it was thought possible, but in the 21st century that kind of slight-of-hand can easily be debunked.

Hubert flipped to the back of the book. "Here's where it gets even crazier."

A folded piece of paper was tucked into the pages. I opened what looked like a torn page from a diary.

The hand-written note read:

Tuesday

Failed to find Wickagua. Found only deforestation. Tribal home is now an oil drilling site. Lake drained. Collecting water samples now impossible.

Wednesday

Hiked deeper into jungle. No sign of natives. Feel a grave injustice has been done.

Thursday

Preparing for home. Found this . . .

Then came the *real* shocker. A Polaroid snapshot was stapled to the note. The image showed the same mirror in the 100-year-old photo leaning against a bulldozer.

"Look closer," said Hubert. Taking a magnifying glass from his pocket, he held it over the photo. I squinted my eyes. The man taking the picture was reflected in the mirror. That man was *Ravi!*

The hospital admitting nurse welcomed me, then sat down at her computer. "Patient's name, please."

"Alec Hakeem," I said.

"When was he admitted?"

"Sometime last night."

All I wanted was Alec's hospital room number. Then I would decide if it was a good idea to even see him. Needless to say, our last meeting didn't go so well. Seeing me might remind him of the humiliation I caused him. Then again, clearing the air might just be what he needs. I'm no psychologist, but a little morale boosting never hurt anybody.

"I'm sorry," said the nurse, looking up from her computer, "no one by that name was admitted here last night."

"Not even to the Emergency Room?"

She typed on her keyboard. "He didn't come through Emergency, either."

"How about Intensive Care?"

More typing. "I've searched the hospital database for the entire week. No one named Hakeem has been here. Maybe he was admitted under another name."

Why would Ravi do that, unless Hakeem really *wasn't* his last name? Just because I saw it on his business card, I shouldn't have accepted it as fact.

I was a pretty poor detective. For all I knew, the nurse was lying to me, or someone had tampered with the hospital records. Agatha Christie endowed her characters with the ability to separate fact from fiction. If only I could get inside her head, maybe I could get somewhere.

"Is there another hospital where he might have been taken?" I asked.

"The only other is the VA, but they don't take emergencies."

A drive over to the VA hospital confirmed what the nurse had said. Their records showed Alec's time spent recovering from his war wounds, and nothing more.

A hand-lettered sign hung in the barbershop window:

CLOSED
All appointments canceled
until further notice.

It was just after lunchtime when I unlocked the front door. Entering the empty shop, I saw the door to the secure hallway standing ajar. I could hear Ravi at work in the lab. I should have gone in there to ask him about his note in Hubert's book, but there were more important questions to consider first. For one, what had become of Alec? Why did his ambulance fail to reach the hospital? If he was indeed missing, why wasn't Ravi out searching for him? (Finally, I was thinking like a real mystery novel sleuth.)

I searched the shop for clues to the answers. I inspected the mirror that had presumably come from the Amazon jungle. I rummaged through some drawers. Being alone, I didn't have to worry about getting caught, until I heard a man's voice say:

"So, you're Amy."

I spun around, ready with excuses to justify my snooping, but no one was there.

"Over here!"

This was getting creepy. Hearing disembodied voices only happens in horror movies.

I sat in the barber chair, and as I waited to hear what the voice would say next, I caught something in the mirror race across the room. "Who's there?"

Staring at my reflection, a man slowly stood up behind my chair. Dressed in a gray suit and tie, I figured him to be a supply salesman, come to replenish Ravi's stockroom.

"Thank goodness," I said. "You scared the bejesus out of me. Should I get Ravi for you?"

But when I turned my head to look back at him, the man was gone, as if vanished by magic. Even spookier, turning back toward the mirror, the reflection showed him still standing behind me!

"How can you be in there, and not be . . . I mean, how is that possible?"

He place his hand on my shoulder. Feeling the touch of his fingers, I glanced down at them, but no hand was there!

"What is this," I said. "I see your reflection, but you're not here to *be* reflected? Are you invisible or something?"

He came around to face me. "Certainly not," he said. "Otherwise you wouldn't see me at all."

"Then, whose hand did I feel on my shoulder?"

"Mine. Everything on your side of the mirror is on my side, too. You felt my hand because you're in *here* with me."

He reached for a spray bottle and picked it up. The same bottle on my side rose into the air, as if being held up by an invisible hand. "Everything in your world is duplicated exactly the same in here. I can move about in my space as you do in yours. The only difference is that everything here is flip-flopped. To you, this bottle reads *Hair Spray*. In here it reads *yarpS riaH*."

"You're not dead, are you?" I asked.

"I'm very much alive, thank you, Amy."

"How do you know my name?"

"Perhaps I should introduce myself. I'm Harley Fink."

This was crazy! I had been looking all over for him, and here he finds me instead. This wasn't quite how I imagined our first meeting. It was like talking through a big hole in the wall to someone in the next room.

"Harley Fink?" I said. "The same one I talked to

on the phone? The same one the police are looking for?"

"In the flesh . . . sort of."

"Does Ravi know you?"

"Very well. He's been removing my guilt for years."

"But how can you be here? You drove off a cliff. You tumbled to the bottom of Grand Gorge. I saw it happen."

"That you did, and by all rights I should be dead. But the Guilt Remover has a handy little side effect. With extreme guilt comes suicidal thoughts. When that happens, you're whisked away into this mirror before you can cause yourself deadly harm. To the outside world, you've simply disappeared."

Alec tried to overdose on pain killers. If Harley was right, then Alec was in that mirror, too. No wonder I couldn't find him.

"Is there any way to get out?" I asked.

"There is! Look in that cupboard above the rinse basin. There you'll find a green bottle."

I opened the cupboard door and found a bottle labeled *Back Splash*.

"Is this it?" I said, holding it up to the mirror.

"Yes. All you have to do is shampoo my hair with it and I'll be outta here."

No question. This was definitely the Wickagua's jungle mirror. Arthur Gimbal claimed that it could bring the dead back to life. Apparently, the *near*

-dead had an all access pass, too.

"How can I shampoo your hair when you're invisible to me?"

"Just watch my reflection. It's easy."

Easy, maybe, but not desirable. Harley Fink had given me no reason to trust him. His lies had turned my world upside down. If I release him from his glass prison, what then? I knew little more about him aside from what I learned from Debbie. But, he was in a rush to get out, and needed my help to do it. That left me an opening for a little tit for tat.

"Is there anyone else in there with you?" I asked.

"You mean Alec?"

"You know him?"

"Of course. I've been watching everything that's gone on in this shop."

"Then you know that he's missing."

"And you think he's in here. He isn't, but I know where to find him. Let me out and I'll tell you where he is."

"Why should I trust you?"

"If you want to see Alec again, you're going to have to."

"Maybe I should bring Ravi out here to check out your story."

He looked me in the eye. "There's something you need to know about him."

"What something?"

"You're not going to like this, Amy. Ravi is the Devil!"

"What are you talking about? He's the nicest man I know—strange, but nice."

"Don't kid yourself. He's a modern-day Dr. Jekyll. You've seen the types of people who come through here: power-hungry politicians, greedy executives, corrupt congressmen—each of them guilty of some grievous act. Do they care? No. Are they ashamed? Of course not. After Ravi removes their guilt, they go back to their fancy offices and do it all over again. They return to their evil ways with a clear conscience."

As much as I wanted to deny it, Harley Fink had raised a valid point. I was already having serious doubts about Ravi's honesty. He misled me into believing that Alec was in the hospital. How many other untruths had he told me?

I stared at the bottle of Back Splash in my hand, unsure what to do, when I heard the door down the hall close.

"You've got to get me out of here, Amy," exclaimed Harley. "Don't let your feelings for Ravi fool you. Consider this: he gave *you* the Guilt Remover without your consent. You may be in here next."

The sound of footsteps echoed down the hall.

"Come back tonight," Harley whispered, then ducked out of sight.

I hid behind the reception desk as Ravi came in. He crossed the room and opened a drawer, then noticed the bottle of Back Splash I had foolishly left on the sink.

Ravi picked it up, then slowly scanned the room. I held my breath as he put the green bottle back in the cupboard. Passing the mirror, he studied its reflection, then went back to his laboratory.

I waited until I heard the lab door close before venturing back out into the shop. It was time I got home. But before leaving, I crept up to the mirror, and whispered, "I'll be back."

Chapter 10

Back Splash

*F*athers of teenage daughters possess a unique gift. A sixth sense kicks in whenever we try to avoid them. I was hoping to keep my after-hours appointment with Harley Fink a secret. Experience told me that my covert operation wouldn't sit well with my dad.

I carefully peered around the kitchen doorway. With his back to me, Dad was leaning over the sink, washing the dinner dishes. With him distracted, I crept quietly to the front door. But just as I reached for the door handle, I heard: "Kind of late to be going out, isn't it, Amy?" Did I mention that dads have eyes in the back of their heads, too?

"I'm just going out for a while," I said.

"Isn't tonight the Junior Prom?"

I pulled a sweatshirt over my head. "I'm not going, remember?"

"Do you mind if I ask where you *are* going?"

Scrutinizing my every move was one of his parental responsibilities. I respected that. Interfering in my mission, however, was something I couldn't allow. If Dad knew what I was up to, I would be grounded for who knows how long. I hoped that I wouldn't have to deceive him, but saving Alec was simply too important.

Dad leaned against the kitchen door frame, drying his hands on a towel. I prepared myself for a thorough inquiry, but instead he gave me an unexpected smile.

"No need," he said. "Have a good time," then went back to his dishes.

I was shocked and relieved at the same time. Rarely was I permitted to go anywhere without a drawn-out description of my planned activities. For some reason, tonight I was free to go my own way. This was way to easy.

I stood beside Dad at the sink. "I'm going to a party to do drugs," I said.

"Yeah, right."

"I'm going out to rob a liqueur store."

"Nice try."

"Why are you so trusting of me all of a sudden?"

He turned off the tap. "That's hard to say. Trusting people takes a kind of blind faith. You don't feel 100% comfortable with what they're doing, but you go along with them anyway. You're still young, Amy, but you're not a child. You've got good instincts. I've seen them. That night the police came here. You demanded to see their IDs. I argued the point, but you stood your ground. I admire that."

What a jerk I was. I should have confessed everything to him right then and there. He was being totally up front with me, and I wasn't returning the favor. I felt horrible, but promised myself to tell him everything when all this was over.

I headed out of the kitchen, free to carry on with my operation. But I suddenly felt concern for my dad. I went back over to him. "Are you going to worry about me?"

He looked at me as if it was for the last time. "If I live to be a hundred, I'll always worry about you. It's a curse that comes with being a parent. But there's an old adage about rearing children: *Until you let them spread their wings, they'll never learn to fly on their own.*"

I had waited so long to hear that. I wanted to wrap my grateful arms around him, but I didn't want to turn this into a weepy moment. Fact is, his remark scared me. Soaring skyward toward independence is one thing. Falling back to Earth on your tush is another.

There was a spookiness to the old downtown after dark. Most of the streetlights were burned out. Few people ventured there after sundown, so the city saw no point in fixing them. No light came from Ravi's upstairs apartment, either, indicating that he had retired for the evening.

With the full moon at my back, I quietly inserted my key into the front door lock. Carefully muting the doorbell with my hand, I tiptoed across the threshold. I made certain that the blinds were closed tight before switching on the lights.

"Mr. Fink?" I whispered. "Are you there?"

Harley's face leaned into view in the mirror. "The coast is clear, Amy."

Without hesitation, his mirror-self crossed the room and sat down at the rinse basin. I swung around to see the empty chair recline by itself—just the kind of thing you'd see in an old Invisible Man movie.

The Back Splash was still in the cupboard. Reaching for the bottle, I stopped short just as I was about to pick it up.

"Having second thoughts?" said Harley.

"Are you a terrorist?"

"One thing you should know by now is that I don't do anything that doesn't turn a profit. Terrorism is for ideological fools. It accomplishes nothing."

"What if something goes wrong?"

"It won't. You think I'd put myself through this if I thought it was hazardous?"

He had a point. What did I have to worry about?

The worse that could happen to me was getting wrinkly fingers. Then again, there was no telling what that stuff was made of.

"Maybe I should wear rubber gloves," I said.

"You're stalling. If it won't hurt my scalp, it won't hurt your hands. But it might hurt Alec the longer you take to get me out of here."

That was our deal: rescue Harley, and I find Alec.

I took the bottle down off the shelf, then remembered that Harley had maneuvered a similar-sized bottle.

"Why are you having *me* do this?" I asked. "You could just as easily do it yourself."

"I tried that already. I shampooed my hair with the bottle in here, but all I got was a clean head of hair. I didn't cross over to the other side like I should have. Apparently, what happens in the mirror, stays in the mirror."

Harley leaned his head back. I opened the faucet, then pointed the spray nozzle into the sink. The water splashed off the space where Harley's invisible head was.

"Do you mind not getting water in my eyes?"

"Oops! Sorry."

Focusing on his mirror image, I redirected the spray, and got the hang of it pretty quickly. Feeling invisible wet hair between my fingers was a little harder to get used to.

I uncapped the bottle of Back Splash. "How

much do I use?"

"That I don't know. Better use a fair amount. I'd hate to leave half of me in the mirror from using too little."

I worked the shampoo into his hair. The lather hovered over the empty sink like a soapy cloud.

"Anything happening?" asked Harley.

"Nothing yet."

I rinsed away the suds, and as the shampoo drained off of Harley's head, strands of his hair appeared in its place!

"Here you come!"

His face then slowly faded in. It was like watching a materializing ghost—first a thin vapor, then gradually becoming more solid.

"I see something!" said Harley. "The ceiling! It's blurry, but I can see it."

"Give it a minute. You're eyeballs still look like little fish bowls."

It didn't take long before his whole head had completely transformed. I poked his cheek with my finger. It was real skin!

He rolled his eyes toward me. "I can see perfectly now. Where's the rest of me?"

"Be patient. Your shoulders are just coming through now."

Little by little, from his neck downward, his body solidified. And when I saw the shine on the tips of his shoes, I knew the job was complete.

"Done!"

I wrapped Harley's head in a towel. He immediately ran over to the mirror. I now saw both Harley *and* his reflection.

"I'll be damned!" he said, toweling his hair dry.

"How do you feel?"

"Refreshed, like I just came from a dip in the ocean."

He picked up a comb and dragged it over his head, then made a troubling comment: "Gotta look good for our guests."

"What do you mean, guests?"

I heard the flip of a switch. The stairway light to Ravi's apartment came on. "Who's down there?" called out Ravi.

The sound of footsteps on the stairs followed.

"What do we do?" I said frantically.

"Let me handle this."

Ravi entered the shop in his bathrobe, and seeing Harley Fink, said, "So! You *were* in the mirror all along."

"I have been ever since my accident."

"How did you get out?"

I lowered my eyes as Ravi looked over at me.

"Amy . . . You?"

Ravi's look of disappointment wounded me like an arrow through the heart.

"You should have told the police about me when they questioned you," said Harley. "They've been following Amy hoping she would lead them to a terrorist. You were already a suspect. All they need now is the evidence to link you to the attempted bombing."

That "fink!" He was out to frame Ravi from the beginning. He had tricked me into believing that he was the victim, when all along he was the aggressor.

"Your evil plan won't work," said Ravi.

"Oh, won't it? I've been watching you. I followed you around the shop unnoticed. I know all about your laboratory. I even know the security code for opening the door."

He strolled over to the front window and peeked through the blinds, then with a flick of his wrist, he unlocked the front door. Flinging it wide open, in charged a dozen policemen with guns drawn.

"Freeze!" shouted the lead officer. We immediately put our hands up—all but Harley, of course.

"What is this?" protested Ravi.

Through the open door marched my chubby friend from the FBI: Policeman #1. "Don't you know a police raid when you see one?" He placed a search warrant in Ravi's raised hand. "Here's my invitation."

"On what grounds have you the right to break into my shop?"

"Suspicion of plotting a terrorist attack." He took his eyes off Ravi and nodded to me. "Fancy finding you here, Amy. Get any unusual phone calls lately?"

His arrogance pisssed me off. I prepared to counter his rudeness with a verbal attack of my own, but not wanting to get any deeper into trouble, I simply said, "Go on a diet, flatfoot!"

His lanky partner, Policeman #2, came through the door and walked over to Harley, asking, "Where's the goods?"

Harley pulled a slip of paper from his coat pocket. "First door down the hall—and here's the security code."

Snapping his fingers, #1 sent two of his officers to inspect the laboratory. He signaled the others to holster their weapons, then told us, "You can put your hands down."

"Can't this wait till morning?"asked Ravi.

"Mr. Fink tipped us off that you were leaving the country tonight."

Harley pointed to the mirror while leaning in to Ravi. "Great cell phone reception in there."

The first cop returned from the lab. "It's like a terrorist's playground in there," he said.

He handed two glass jars over to #2. He opened the first jar, sniffed its contents, and said, "Sodium Hydroxophene. A high-explosive compound."

"It also removes fingernail polish," Ravi added.

Sniffing in the second jar, #2 said, "Ammonium Perkacide. A detonation agent."

"For disinfecting hair brushes."

The second cop came out of the lab with a large cardboard box, "Sir, we also found *this*." Tipping it over, a mountain of paper money spilled out onto the floor.

"Those are legitimate earnings," said Ravi. "I can't conduct my research without funding."

"The court will be happy to hear all about it," said #1. He handcuffed Ravi. "You're under arrest for possession of banned substances, operating an illegal research laboratory, and—oh, yes—the attempted bombing of the Wild Things Survival Fund."

"I've done nothing wrong! Tell them, Amy. For God's sake! Tell them how my work will benefit people."

What good would that have done? Harley Fink had engineered the perfect frame-up, and I was his unwitting accomplice.

#1 dragged his prisoner to the front door like he was an animal. Ravi looked back at me with sorrowful eyes, as if he had been betrayed by his best friend. In a way, I guess he had.

#2 called to his men, "Load this terrorist bum into the patrol car and read him his rights." He turned to me. "And don't you go too far, miss. You'll be wanted for questioning."

The front door slammed with a bang! leaving Harley and I alone in the empty shop.

"Alright, you!" I said. "You got what you wanted. I

held up my end of the bargain. Where's Alec?"

"Alec? Who's Alec?"

My face reddened with rage. "You lying scum!"

"Lighten up, kid. Just what did you expect? I'm a scoundrel and a cheat. I told you so that night on the phone."

"Why are you being such an a-hole? What's got you so pissed off that you have to put Ravi behind bars?"

"If you must know, some of Ravi's wealthy clients, including me, learned of his intent to publicize the Guilt Remover. Going public with that information would shine a light on us, too. All of our illegal activities would be exposed. Fortunes would be wiped out. We'd face certain jail time. I'm afraid we couldn't permit that to happen."

"You're forgetting about *me*. Aren't you afraid I'll tell the police what I know?"

Harley laughed. "You *try* telling them. Tell them all about secret shampoos and magic mirrors. And if by some miracle someone believes you, we have ways of shutting people up. We're ruthless, Amy. We take what we want."

"And for that you'd deprive the world of the greatest achievement in medicine since penicillin?"

"In a nutshell, yes."

I raised my hand to slap his face, but he grabbed hold of my wrist.

"For what it's worth," he said, "I agree with you.

Ravi's discovery *would* have been a great boon to mankind." He opened the front door, and just before closing it behind him, said, "See? I'm really not such a heartless guy."

I plopped down in the barber chair and thought back to what led me there in the first place. I began this adventure with one goal in mind: find my mystery caller. And despite everything else that happened, I had done just that. Mission Accomplished! Game over.

As for Alec and Ravi, well, where does it say that I have to solve everyone's problems? For sure, I did the best I could, and should walk away proud of that.

Now I can tell my dad everything—only, I couldn't. I knew just what he'd say: "What did you do, Amy, quit? You let that bully Fink walk all over you?"

No, this *wasn't* game over! If only to live up to my father's expectations, I had to forge ahead. I couldn't let him down. More importantly, I couldn't let *myself* down. Who was I kidding? I missed Ravi. I missed Alec. But what could I do? Harley Fink had the situation sewn up so tightly that no one could unravel it.

Then, a faint sound broke my concentration. A cell phone was ringing. I glanced around the shop, turning my head and listening. The counter seemed a likely place to find it. Nope, not there. I pulled opened some drawers as the phone kept ringing. Then, I discovered that it *was* on the counter—the counter inside the *mirror!*

Mr. "I take what I want" had been shampooed back to reality without his phone! If its call history hadn't been deleted, it would reveal unshakable proof that he had called me, placing him smack dab in the middle of his own treachery. Ravi would be in the clear.

I suddenly felt invigorated. The party was just getting started.

There was only one hitch: the phone was on the other side of the mirror. I paced back and forth in front of it like a caged lion. It seemed so close that I foolishly reached for it, bumping my knuckles against the glass. What I needed was some expert help—a science wiz who understood chemistry, physics, and the laws of time and space.

Hubert!

Chapter 11

The Prom

*R*evolving search lights beamed into the night sky, like the ones you see at Hollywood premieres. The only thing was, this wasn't Tinseltown. It wasn't even California. It was Shankstonville, and the bright lights were welcoming guests to my high school's Junior Prom.

Holding this elegant affair in the school gymnasium had the whole Junior Class up in arms. They would have preferred a posh ballroom in a swanky hotel, but their fundraising efforts hadn't brought in enough cash to afford anything that nice. So, their limited resources went to buying Hawaiian leis and plastic tiki gods, all to enhance the prom's theme, *Paradise in the Tropics*.

Chaperoning the event was Miss Tuttle, our school's lone female P.E. teacher. She was extremely athletic, and was more muscular than the men in her department. Those unlucky students who were assigned to her class prepared for a rough semester. Through rigorous exercise and long-distance running, she was obsessed with slimming down the fast-food generation.

The prom was well underway by the time I arrived. A few latecomers were lined up at the front door. They looked so good in their evening formals: girls in satin gowns and boys in velvet tuxedoes. I was in sneakers and jeans, but then, I hadn't come to join the party. Hubert was in the gym, and I needed to see him.

Miss Tuttle greeted the prom guests cordially, only refusing entry to those who had clearly been abusing the Bottle. Though nicely dressed, seeing the brawny teacher in formalwear was like seeing Arnold Schwarzenegger in drag.

As my turn came, Miss Tuttle took one look at my shabby attire, and said, "Does that outfit come with a corsage?"

"I'm not here for the prom," I said. "I need to talk to someone inside. It'll just take a minute."

"Not dressed like that, you won't!"

"But it's important."

"So is preserving the dignity of the Junior Prom. Those kids in there are building lifelong memories, and I'm not going to have you spoil it for them. Go home and put on a dress and I'll let you in."

"There isn't time for that."

I charged the doorway, but Miss Tuttle's broad

frame blocked my way.

"Honor the dress code or take a hike!" she demanded.

I grumbled while slowly walking away, keeping Miss Tuttle in view. I waited for her to welcome the next arrivals, then dashed around to the side of the building. Tugging on the exit door handles, they all seemed to be locked. I knocked quietly on each one but got no response. Pounding on them would have produced better results, but I didn't want to draw attention to myself.

Finally, the latch on the last door clicked. I pulled it open, unaware that someone inside was leaning against it. Out tumbled Garrett Kaminsky, the most popular boy in school. Garrett was the dreamy type who could melt a girl's heart just by winking at her. He was also captain of the football team and a notorious party animal.

His fall to the ground must not have hurt him much, because he was on his back laughing hysterically, yelling, "Touchdown!" And no wonder. His breath smelled like a liqueur store after an earthquake.

"Congratulations, Garrett!" I said, stepping over him. "You got past Miss Tuttle. Not an easy task."

I started to close the door, when he looked up at me through bloodshot eyes. "Don't shut that!" he cried. "You lock me out and she'll bust me for sure."

I leaned over the inebriated boy. Brushing away the dirt from his white dinner jacket, I said, "I'd love to help you out. I really would. But we must preserve the dignity of the Junior Prom."

I slipped inside and shut the door, locking it behind me.

Keeping to the shadows, I looked out over the tropical setting. The prom committee had created an enchanting, romantic atmosphere. Tiki torches burned bright with artificial flames. Bring your date a cupful of Hawaiian punch from a grass-covered wet bar. Feast on Polynesian fare at tables graced with lovely orchid centerpieces. And, what prom would be complete without a rotating mirror ball on the ceiling. The whole room sparkled from its tiny points of light, sweeping across walls and over smiling faces.

Everyone was having such a good time. A group teetering on a surfboard laughed, while posing for a souvenir selfie. Girls cheered their dates as they competed in a limbo contest. Couples embraced while slow-dancing to the mellow sound of strumming ukuleles.

The focal point of the prom was a mock luau staged in the center of the gym. Roasting real pigs inside public buildings was prohibited under local fire codes. Instead, a lavish buffet was provided by a caterer. The savory aroma of teriyaki and grilled mahi-mahi made my mouth water.

Peeking around a coconut tree, I spotted Hubert, sitting alone at a linen-draped table. He looked so sad—and I felt so ashamed. I should have come with him to the prom like he wanted me to.

I crept closer, then while no one was looking, snuck over and sat in a vacant chair next to him.

He was startled by my sudden appearance. "Amy! What are you—"

"Shh!" I whispered. "You have to come with me. I need your help."

"What? Now?"

"Right now!"

On the table sat a crystal bowl filled with cocktail peanuts. The hectic day had left me little time to eat. "Mind if I have some?" I said, dipping my fingers into the snack food.

"What do you mean coming here like this? I can't leave now."

"Sure you can. It's not like you're with someone."

Just then, I spotted Lydia Hobbs heading in our direction, strutting her stuff for everyone to see, like she always does.

"Oh, no!" I said. "You and *Lydia?*"

"Why the surprise? You were there when I asked her out."

"Yeah, but I never imagined she'd go through with it." Lydia was getting closer. "Listen to me, Hubert. You *have* to do this. I'll explain later."

"What do I tell my date?"

"Make up an excuse." I grabbed a handful of peanuts and jumped behind a fern.

Lydia arrived a moment later, looking spectacular in her low-cut, high-slit gown. Like a perfect gentleman, Hubert stood up and pulled out her chair for her.

"How about a refill on that shrimp cocktail?" she said.

I threw a peanut at Hubert's head. He slapped the back of his neck.

"What was that for?" asked Lydia.

"Nothing. I mean. . . okay, I'll get you some more shrimp."

I tossed another peanut, this time hitting Hubert's ear.

"Stop that!" he blurted out.

Lydia looked at him funny. "Is there something wrong with you?"

"Just an itch. It's one of those little nuisances that won't go away." He looked in my direction. "Like someone I know."

Mistaking his remark as intended for her, Lydia said, "You know, Hubert, if you want to get rid of me, just say so."

Hubert stood up and bowed. "Will you excuse me a moment?"

I followed Hubert to the buffet table where I pulled him aside. I can't remember when I had seen him more pissed. "You've got exactly thirty seconds to explain yourself."

I pointed to his table. "I can't believe you came with *her!*"

"You turned me down."

"I know I did, but she's so out of your league."

"Look, she may be a bimbo, but she *is* my date, and I'm not leaving without her."

I narrowed my eyes at him. "I'm going over and tell Lydia what you just said."

Hubert grabbed my arm. "Wait! How long will this take?"

"Not long. I'll have you back before they crown the Prom Queen."

Hubert made up a flimsy excuse to tell Lydia. Not being terribly creative, he said his mom had called to say that his pet hamster was having convulsions. He needed to get home immediately, but promised a speedy return to the prom. Not surprisingly, Lydia bought his story.

"Where are we going?" said Hubert, behind the wheel of his SUV.

"To the 2-Bit Solution barbershop," I said.

"Okay, let's have it. What's so important that you have to abduct me?"

So far, Hubert knew about the barbershop, its secret laboratory, the Guilt Remover, Ravi, Harley, and Alec. Believing all that required him to take a huge leap of faith. I wasn't sure how much more wackiness he was willing to take.

"Get out your spoonful of sugar," I said, "you're gonna find this hard to swallow."

"Try me!"

I told him that Ravi's mirror can kidnap you.

"Sound crazy?"

"Coming from you, it makes perfect sense."

I explained that suicidal thoughts send you there.

"Believe me?"

"What's not to believe."

I told him that the Back Splash was the only way out of it.

"Still with me?"

"Absolutely. But how do you know it works?"

"I've done it. I shampooed someone back to reality, but I made one little mistake: I backsplashed Satan into the world."

"Why am I not surprised? Who is this demon?"

"Harley Fink."

Hubert flashed me a huge grin. "That's great! Now the cops can pick him up and they'll stop harassing you."

"They already had their chance for that. Instead, they arrested Ravi and let Harley walk free."

"I sense that something is amiss."

"You might say that. But there's still a chance to set things right. When I shampooed Harley back, he left his phone behind in the mirror. It's the phone he used to call me on."

"So, what's your plan?"

"Get the phone. The data on it will clear Ravi of all wrongdoing and put Harley Fink behind bars where he belongs."

"But you said it's in the mirror. How are we supposed to get it back? It'll take a genius to figure that out."

I plopped my hand down on Hubert's shoulder. "Welcome to my world, Mr. Wizard."

Chapter 12

Breaking and Entering

*H*ubert doused his headlights and cut the engine as we rolled up to the barbershop. I had only been gone for an hour, and expected to find the shop the way I left it, but the police had other ideas. Yellow crime tape now stretched around the entire building. Plywood sheets covered the doors and windows. A bright red and orange warning sign was pasted on the front door:

DANGER!
BIOHAZARD
Entering these premises will lead to
arrest and prosecution.

The authorities must have thought the sign was enough to secure the building, because there wasn't a cop in sight.

"Well, it's been nice hangin' with ya," said Hubert.

"I'm going back to the prom."

"Can't you see what they're doing?" I said. "There's nothing hazardous in there. They're just trying to keep looters and looky-loos away."

"Okay, smarty. Let's assume it *is* safe, how do you plan to get inside?"

The empty building next door was the former home of Beacon Records. The music superstore was once a popular hangout for people of all musical tastes. Like most vinyl record sellers, it suffered a slow death in the age of the digital download.

The store was gone, but the building still had some usefulness left in it. Around the back we discovered a rooftop access ladder. We also found that the police had failed to batten down Ravi's 2nd floor window.

"Here's what we're going to do," I said. "We climb the ladder to Beacon's roof, cross over to Ravi's building, then climb down the fire escape to the 2nd floor. All we have to do then is jimmie open the window and we're in."

"That's breaking and entering," said Hubert. "People get arrested for that."

"Not if they don't get caught."

"I say it's too dangerous."

"I say it's worth the risk."

"Is there any point in arguing with you?"

"Not really."

Hubert grabbed the sides of the metal ladder and gave it a firm shake. "Looks sturdy enough." He then removed his tuxedo jacket and hung it on a nail. "Gonna need my rental deposit money for posting bail."

Hubert went first, scurrying up the ladder like a cat up a tree. Safely on the roof, he waved for me to join him. I started up slowly, grabbing each rusty rung tightly. Not being too fond of high places, I was careful not to look down.

Making it to the roof wasn't that difficult, but it was tiring. Taking a moment to catch our breath, Hubert's cell phone rang.

"It's a text from Lydia," he said. "She's asking when I'm coming back. How do I reply?"

"You don't," I said. "You're going to pretend you didn't get her message, and if she asks why, you were out of signal range."

Being in charge is a great feeling. I was the commander and chief strategist. My plan was moving along nicely, until an unexpected hitch abruptly halted our progress. A four-foot alleyway separated the two buildings.

"Hmm," said Hubert, looking over the edge. "Looks like we're gonna have to jump over it."

I was afraid he would say that. The thought of leaping over that divide terrified me. Hubert had tried to warn me that this was a task better suited for Spiderman, but I wouldn't listen.

My stomach sank as I stared down into the chasm below.

"What's the matter, Amy? You look a little pale."

"We're two stories up," I said nervously.

"Don't think of it that way. If I drew a four-foot chalk line on the sidewalk, you could jump it end to end easy. Just imagine you're on the ground."

"Well . . . alright." I backed up to get a running start.

"Keep your eyes on the other side," advised Hubert.

Mentally I was ready for the challenge, but my shaking body didn't want to cooperate.

"I can't do it!"

Hubert pointed his index finger in the air, like holding a starting pistol. "It's the Olympic long jump finals. Clear four feet and the gold medal is ours. Your country is counting on you!"

You're not a child, my dad had told me that very night. He proclaimed his faith in my judgment and courage. Now, it was time to prove that I was made of the Right Stuff.

"On your mark . . . get set . . . bang!"

I sprinted across the rooftop and jumped, like my legs were made out of bedsprings. Tumbling onto Ravi's roof, I had made it across—with an extra three feet to spare!

"Bravo!" cheered Hubert.

Brushing myself off, I yelled back to him,

"Your turn!"

As Hubert backed up to start his run, he looked down at his feet. "Oh, look what I found!" A wooden scaffolding plank was laying up there the whole time. He placed it across the gap like a bridge and leisurely crossed over to me.

"I swear I didn't know it was there," he said.

Yeah, right!

We easily climbed the fire escape down one floor. The only obstacle left was an old-style casement window. I cupped my hands around my eyes and peered through the glass, finding a kitchen sink just on the other side. Jamming my fingers under the window's wooden frame, I pulled up on it, but it wouldn't budge.

"Looks like your plan has hit another snag," said Hubert. "It's locked from the inside."

Again, Hubert's phone sounded its annoying ringtone. "Shut that thing off!" I insisted, but Hubert tuned me out while staring at the screen.

"I am so screwed!" he said. "Lydia was just crowned Queen of the Junior Prom."

"Goody!" I said. "Now, help me open this blamed window."

Hubert pulled a credit card from his wallet and slid it under the window frame, unlatching the inside lock.

"Where did you learn that?" I asked.

"James Bond. He did it in that movie you refused

to go see with me."

Crawling over a sink full of dirty dishes, we finally made it into the dark apartment. I stopped Hubert just as he was about to switch on the lights. We didn't need a passing patrol car to report a lit room in an uninhabited building. Fortunately, a flashlight from a kitchen drawer provided all the light we needed.

I shined it down the darkened staircase, as we slowly tiptoed the creaky steps to the ground floor.

To make sure the shop was empty, I shined the light in every corner of the room, then pointed it at the mirror.

"There it is," I whispered.

We huddled close together as we crept toward it. The squeaking of Hubert's dress shoes sliced through the stillness. Then, we both jumped from the sudden blare of a cell phone ringing. Hubert tapped on his phone's screen, but the noise continued. He tapped it again and again. "Why doesn't the blasted thing stop?"

"Here's why," I said. "Look!"

In the beam of my flashlight was Harley Fink's phone, ringing on the other side of the mirror. Hubert instinctively reached in to shut it off, banging his knuckles on the glass.

"What the hell *is* this!" he said.

"What I've been trying to tell you. The phone is locked inside that mirror, and there's only one way to get it out." I dug a straight razor out of a drawer.

Seeing the threatening object, Hubert threw his hands up. "What are you going to do?"

"Relax. I'm only going to slit my wrist."

The phone's ringing continued.

"Are you out of your friggin' mind?" said Hubert.

"It's okay. The mirror will take me before anything bad happens. Once I'm in there, and have the phone, you'll shampoo me back out. Understand?"

Hubert grabbed the blade. "Let the mirror take *me.*"

I seized it back. "It has to be me. I've used the Guilt Remover. You haven't."

As we struggled over the shaving razor, the ringing stopped. Inside the mirror, Harley's phone was resting in the palm of someone's hand—*Alec's* hand!

"I knew you were in there!" I said excitedly. "Are you alright?"

"I'd be a lot better if someone got me outta here," said Alec.

Perturbed, Hubert said, "You must be Alec, the one whose been causing Amy so much grief."

Alec replied pleasantly, "And you must be Hubert, her trusting friend."

"Do you realize all the trouble you've caused?"

"Sorry about that. No hard feelings."

Alec offered to shake hands, but Hubert hadn't

yet grasped the concept of the one-way reflection. Again, he thumped his fingers against the mirror.

Seeing Alec safe warmed my heart, but I couldn't be sure he was so glad to see me. A lot of bitterness was exchanged the last time we were together. But as he chatted with Hubert, he face me, and his forgiving smile seemed to be saying, "Don't sweat it."

While the boys got better acquainted, I went to the cupboard where I last saw the Back Splash. As I reached for the door handle, I looked down into the rinse basin. The bottle was laying at the bottom of the sink. The cap had been removed. I turned the bottle upside down. It was empty!

Suddenly, the lights came on, and standing by the wall switch was Harley Fink, holding Hubert's tuxedo jacket. "Does this belong to anyone?"

"You sneak!" I said. "You've been following us."

"I'm surprised at you, Amy," said Harley. "Did you really think you were the only one after that phone? I was out celebrating when I realized it was missing. I knew I had left it in the mirror. I suspected that you knew it, too, and would be coming back for it."

"Who is this man?" asked Alec.

Harley stepped up to the mirror. "We haven't been properly introduced. Harley Fink's the name. I'm the one who put your father in jail. Everyone says he's a terrorist, but don't believe everything you hear. You see, I'm the one who planted the bomb, forced Ravi to take the fall, then tricked Amy into shampooing me out of the mirror. My performance was flawless. Leaving my phone behind was my only screwup. Now, I've returned to the scene of the crime to reclaim it."

"Where's the Back Splash?" I demanded.

"The sewer. While you were chatting with your little friends, I poured it down the sink."

"Not a very bright move," said Hubert. "With no Back Splash, that phone is as much out of your reach as it is ours."

Harley stroked his chin in thought. "You know, you're absolutely right. Best to leave it where it is." He picked up my receptionist chair and lifted it over his head. "And, to make sure it stays there . . ."

He took aim at the mirror as Hubert jumped into action. He tried to wrestled the chair away from him, but Harley was stronger. I was about to join the fight, when a voice spoke from the back of the room:

"Smile, Daddy!"

The struggle for the chair ended as we all turned toward the sound. It was Debbie Fink, pointing her smartphone at her dad. The phone's glowing orange light went out as she tapped on the screen. "And . . . saved to the cloud."

"What did you just do?" asked Harley.

"Caught on camera, as they say on TV. I recorded

your whole confession, and saved the file where you can't get at it."

With Harley frozen in fear, Hubert easily removed the chair from his grip.

Debbie tucked her phone into her back pocket. "You should have come to my graduation, Dad."

"I wanted to go, sweetpea," said Harley, with arms open. "Honest!"

"That's not what I've heard. While I was getting my diploma, you were somewhere at the bottom of Grand Gorge."

"What are you going to do with that video?"

"Nothing. Think of it as my own little insurance policy. It guarantees that you won't miss any more of my special days."

"That's blackmail!"

"So it is. Hmm. Must be a genetic thing." She smiled sweetly and took hold of Harley's arm. "After you, Daddy. I want to tell you about the new car I've had my eye on."

Sending Harley up the stairs, Debbie turned to me. "Sorry to put you through all this," she said. "Hope I can make it up to you someday."

"Nothing to feel sorry for," I said. "You saved the mirror. If only you could have saved the Back Splash, too."

"Don't be so negative. There must be more around here someplace. Besides, where there's love, there's hope." She winked at Alec, then joined her dad up the stairs.

Hubert gave me a puzzled look. "What did she mean by *that?*" He then scowled at Alec.

"Calm yourself, ol' buddy," said Alec. "Amy's heart doesn't belong to me. Now, if you're finished with this soap opera, you'll find more Back Splash in the lab."

Alec would soon be back in the real world, along with Harley Fink's phone. The incriminating evidence we had hoped to find on it was intact. I couldn't wait to tell Ravi.

Kicking down the plywood door, we stepped outside. Alec tugged on the yellow crime tape. "Don't like the idea of sleeping at a crime scene," he said.

"Where will you stay tonight, then?" asked Hubert.

"At my house," I insisted. "My parents are very liberal-minded about these things."

"Thanks," said Alec, "but that won't be necessary. The VA has a bed ready for me whenever I need one." He breathed in the cool night air. "Freedom never tasted sweeter. Thanks, you two. I owe you, big time."

The drive to the VA hospital gave us time to talk. With situations explained and apologies accepted, we were all friends again.

We said our curbside good-byes in front of Alec's temporary home, and as Hubert and I drove off, his phone signaled another incoming text. "It's Lydia."

> GETTING RIDE HOME WITH
> GARRETT KAMINSKY.
> SOBERING HIM UP. LOL :)

Chapter 13

Squirrelly

*L*ike a swarm of attacking locust, the media descended on our little farming town. Capturing a terrorist in small-town America was big news. TV furnished the fear. Radio supplied the rage. Tabloids provided the blame. *If it happened here, it can happen anywhere* was the dominant theme.

Social media was especially brutal. Cell phone video of Ravi in handcuffs went viral. Angry tweets demanded that all Middle Easterners be deported. Radical websites tried and convicted Ravi online, even before any details were released.

TV satellite trucks grabbed up all the prime downtown parking spots. The fast-spreading fury was bound to escalate into violence, and the producers wanted to capture every minute of it.

The locals didn't disapoint them. Demonstrators took up positions outside the barbershop. A mob of angry protesters gathered at one end of the street, shouting, *Muslims go home!* At the other end were men in long robes and women in hijabs, proclaiming, *We are not terrorists!*

What was happening to our humble little community? Our tolerant townsfolk, who had shown such hospitality toward their immigrant neighbors, had turned into vicious animals. But whether you were a hatemonger or a pacifist, everyone turned out to watch the media circus—including me.

Shankstonville's own *Eyewitness News* team was on scene, too. The rooftop antenna on its TV news van was extended in preparation for a live report. And as the technical crew unloaded their mobile studio, out stepped Mr. Lewis, the station's News Director.

He mixed in with the crowd, searching for someone willing to comment on the situation. He must have thought that interviewing a teenager would attract a younger audience, because he approached *me*.

This was a bad move on his part. I had once begged Mr. Lewis to report on my young niece's sudden disappearance. He refused, stating that simply being missing wasn't sensational enough. Unless she had been murdered or assaulted, he wasn't about to disrupt his precious programming schedule. Now I saw a chance for a little payback. Fortunately for me, his recollection of that meeting had long faded.

"Good afternoon," he said. "Mr. Lewis, WSVL-TV. Mind If I ask you a few questions?"

"Not at all," I replied.

"What's your take on the recent terrorist arrest?"

"Nobody likes a terrorist."

"How do you feel about the protests?"

"Free speech: you gotta love it!"

"May I interview you on camera?"

"Absolutely! I'll give you the most honest answers I can."

Mr. Lewis pressed on his earpiece, listening to the director back at the station. *Breaking News!* whirled onto a small video monitor resting at the cameraman's feet.

"Standby!"

As the camera's red tally light lit up, this is what the TV viewers saw:

Mr. Lewis nodded to the camera.

"I'm here in downtown Shankstonville. As you can see behind me, demonstrators have assembled, outraged that a terrorist has been living in their midst. As fear grips this sleepy midwestern town, its citizens have taken to the streets in protest. Let's get some local reaction."

The camera panned over to me.

"How does it feel knowing that a terrorist

has been living in your own backyard?"
asked Lewis.

"*Suspected* . . . terrorist," I said firmly.
"Suspected!"

"Yes, of course. But learning that a
bomber has been lurking in the shadows—"

"*Alleged* . . . bomber. In this country, a
person is 'alleged' to have done something
until it is proven."

I batted my eyelashes at him like a
character in a Bugs Bunny cartoon. His
embarrassment showed as he turned back to
the camera.

"Clearly, tensions have left these tormented
townsfolk in shock. Back to you in the
studio."

"Clear!"

I could tell that Mr. Lewis wasn't pleased with
my performance. "Thanks for nothin', kid!"

"Always happy to serve the Media," I said.

Coiling his microphone cable, he suddenly
remembered who I was. "Wait a minute! Don't I
know you?"

Boom! Boom! Boom!

A sudden burst of gunfire sent people scattering
in all directions. Women shrieked in terror. I
instinctively dropped to the ground. Lewis
instinctively didn't—grabbing his cameraman and

racing toward the disturbance. Everyone was panic-stricken, all except Snipper Jim, standing in front of his shop, casually inhaling on a cigarette.

As an all-out brawl erupted between the rival protesters, Jim waved me over to him. I darted across the street, hunched over like an infantryman ducking enemy fire.

"Best hullabaloo this town's had in years," said Jim.

"I've never seen anything like it," I said. "What are they all so mad about?"

"Not mad. Scared."

I jumped behind Jim as a flying beer bottle shattered on the sidewalk next to us. "They don't look so scared to me."

"They're not afraid of buttin' heads, that's for sure. No, it's what they don't understand that really scares 'em. Strangers move into town lookin' different—skin different, church different. So, the locals whip up a firestorm to drive 'em out. I've seen it a hundred times before. Crazy thing is, they think it'll make things better, but it don't."

"Since when did you get so smart?"

"Don't know about that. Jus' know human nature. Can't succeed in business if you don't know how people think."

"What success? Your salon is always empty."

Jim laughed. "Let the damn thing fail. Got a new enterprise that's a real money-maker. Want to see it?"

The back room of Jim's shop was filled with wooden pallets, stacked high with hundreds of shipping cartons. He opened one box and pulled out a shampoo bottle. Its label read, *Guilt-Be-Gone!*

The product name was eerily similar to Ravi's Guilt Remover—too similar to be a coincidence.

"What's that used for?" I asked Jim.

"Like it says on the label: *Lather it on, and guilt be gone!*"

"I knew it! You stole Ravi's secret shampoo!"

"Take it easy! You should be thankin' me. With Ravi in the slammer, how're people gonna know about it?"

"Don't give me that. You've twisted an important discovery into a cheesy novelty to make a quick buck."

"That's your take. The way I see it, I'm providing a public service. A lot of people really need this stuff, and now they can get it—and at only $500 a bottle!"

I was so mad I couldn't see straight. If only I had an ax I could smash Jim's dastardly scheme to pieces. But it was too late for that.

I bolted out of Jim's front door and ran to the alley behind Ravi's shop. The padlock to the metal storage container had been cut off. Forcing open the heavy door, it was completely empty. Not a drop of Guilt Remover was left.

In disbelief, I walked in to the middle of the

container, then heard the wailing of rusty hinges. A loud *clunck!* echoed through the hollow shell. I had been shut inside!

Fumbling in the dark, I felt around for an inside latch, but couldn't find one. I placed my ear against the wall and heard footsteps running away.

"Jim, you sleazeball," I shouted, "open this door!" I listened for a response, but heard none. I banged on the door. "Someone get me the hell outta here!"

Being so far off the street, I worried that my cries for help were being drowned out by the noisy demonstration. Droplets of sweat formed on my forehead. I hoped that I wouldn't get broiled like a steak from the afternoon heat. Luckily, I didn't have to worry about suffocating. A slim ray of light streamed in through a tennis ball-sized hole in the roof.

I sat down on the dusty floor and waited for someone to happen by. What else was there to do?

How long I would be stuck in that metal dungeon was impossible to tell. My mind wandered to the plight of coal miners trapped underground. What were their thoughts while waiting to be rescued? How did they handle the possibility of not getting saved at all?

Just then, the sunlight coming through the ceiling flickered. I immediately looked up. "Is somebody there?" But It wasn't the shadow of my rescuer. It was an intruder. A little brown squirrel had squeezed through the opening, temporarily blocking out the light.

With cheeks bulging, he scurried down the wall, then crossed over to a corner. There he unloaded his cargo under a pile of dry leaves, unconcerned that a human was sharing his hiding place.

"Hey, little fella," I said. "Could you grab someone outside to come let me out? All you have to do is tug on their pants, then lead them back here. You know? Like Lassie does."

The squirrel stood up on his hind feet and gazed at me, as if to say, "Dumb ass! Don't you know you're talking to a squirrel?"

For sure, the boredom and isolation were affecting my reason. I closed my eyes. How ridiculous, I thought, asking for help from a dumb forest creature. It was then that I heard a high-pitched, squeaky voice say:

"Lassie's a dog!"

Okay, I was already a little stir-crazy, but I had sense enough to know that squirrels can't talk. Still, to prove that I wasn't losing my marbles, I opened my eyes and replied, "Say that again."

Chewing on a peanut, the squirrel said, "If you don't mind, I'm trying to eat." He held out his half-eaten treat. "Want some?"

My eyes widened with astonishment. "How is it that you can talk?"

"How is it that you got trapped in this soup can? You're the one with the superior brain."

I pinch the bridge of my nose and shook my head. "This isn't happening."

The little squirrel hopped over to me. "You're so right. Who ever heard of a talking squirrel? A singing chipmunk, perhaps, but never a squirrel that speaks."

"Then, what *are* you?"

"Your conscience, maybe—like Pinnochio's Jiminy Cricket. Or, I might be Gertie, your imaginary childhood friend, returned to keep you company."

"How do you know about Gertie?"

"I know all about you. Squirrels are great observers. Living in trees, we see everything you silly humans do."

"You expect me to believe that? What am I, stupid or something?"

"*Extremely* stupid, or you wouldn't have walked right into Snipper Jim's trap."

"So, I messed up. At least I'm not freaking out over it."

The squirrel rapped on the door with his little knuckles, then mocked me by shouting, "Someone get me the hell outta here!"

I wondered if trapped coal miners experienced the same thing. Just my luck I get a hallucination that enjoys being rude.

"That hurt my feelings," I said.

"Good! Now you know how Hubert felt when you dashed his hopes of taking you out."

"You don't understand. Dating leads to intimacy —leads to commitment—leads to a relationship. Then comes the inevitable breakup. What chance would I have of regaining Hubert's friendship after all that?

"Taking chances is the only path to finding happiness." From his corner stash, he dragged out a Junior Prom ticket stub. "Here was a chance for happiness you should have jumped at."

"Proms are foolish. All that primping and preening, pretending to be something you're not."

"'*Everyone was having such a good time.*' Those were your exact thoughts. Proms are once-in-a-lifetime traditions that no young person should miss."

"You make me sound like a hermit. True, I keep to myself, but I'm perfectly happy that way."

"Blah-blah-blah! You live your life in the dark—just like you're doing now in this oversized lunch box." He ran up the wall and pointed out the hole in the roof. "Out there—in the light—that's where life happens."

"Easy for you. You don't have a two-ton door blocking your way."

"Some doors have to be closed before others will open. He hurried back down and brushed a large heart shape in the dust with his tail. "Try opening *that* for a change."

As much as I hated to hear it, everything that little rodent said was true. I longed to join in the dance, but was too snooty to learn the steps. Love was knocking at my door, while I cowardly watched through the keyhole. I was living a lie. And while I was convinced that I was happy, I was only hurting myself.

The squirrel climbed back up to the ceiling. "Well, gotta go now."

"Wait! Are you just going to leave me here?"

"You've got good instincts, just like our dad said. Use them. You can start by letting yourself out of this heated freight car."

"Aren't you forgetting something? The door's locked."

"But the door *isn't* locked, only stuck. I checked it out."

"Why didn't you say so before?"

"Some people have to learn their lessons the hard way. You're one of them. Put your shoulder to the door next time. You might be surprised at what happens."

A flash of fur and the squirrel was gone.

I stood up and charged at the door like a raging rhinoceros. Throwing my full weight against it, the stubborn thing opened!

I spilled out onto the ground, laughing at the absurdity of it all. Flat on my back, I squinted at the branches in the tree above me. Was that a squirrel I saw? No, just a cooing Mourning Dove, welcoming me back to the natural world. As for animals that talk, inspecting the container showed the dust-covered floor undisturbed. There were no tracks left behind by tiny feet, nor any heart-shaped drawings in the dust.

I came around to the front of Ravi's shop just as the last news van drove away. While I was busy conversing with a squirrel, the police had broken up the demonstration. The rioters had all gone home. With no more disturbing images to broadcast, there was no point in the media sticking around.

Carefully stepping over broken glass, I couldn't tell if I was on a battlefield or in a town hit by a tornado. Nearly all the windows in the buildings had been smashed. A police car had been torched. Ugly slurs were spray-painted on walls.

Where was Ravi's *Hate Slayer* shampoo when we needed it? We could have doused those rabble-rousers with it from a water-dropping helicopter.

When you think about it, it's not that crazy an idea. Those choppers are good at putting out fires in people's backyards. Who knows? One day they might be used to put out the intolerance in people's hearts.

Chapter 14

The Phone

Anyone who watches daytime television knows *The Law Offices of Norman Hampstead*. Find a channel running old 1970s sitcoms, and the personal injury lawyer will be there promoting his law firm. His commercials always begin with him asking,

"Have you or a loved one been injured . . . ?"

After boasting his success rate, he ends by declaring,

"Se habla español."

Hampstead's ads weren't much different from those of his competitors. But unlike the ones who promise huge cash settlements, he actually delivers.

Twisting baseless claims into victories was his specialty. Wake up with a stiff neck and he'll turn it into a work-related injury. Rear-end an old lady's car and he'll make it look like it was her fault.

A former criminal trial lawyer, Hampstead once defended a Wall Street banker accused of fraud. His defense was so compelling that the judge not only acquitted his client, but invested in his latest scam: luxury resorts in Tibet.

"Anything to win" was Hampstead's motto. He was the perfect choice to represent Ravi.

Now that a lawyer was on board, he would need evidence to support his case—and I had the one piece that guaranteed Ravi an acquittal: Harley Fink's cell phone.

Having Failed to enable its password option, Harley had left the door wide open to its internal data. The call records proved conclusively that *he* was the one who called me the night of the police pursuit. This not only meant Ravi's freedom, I, too, would be off the hook, and ol' Mr. Fink would be nailed as the criminal mastermind.

Meanwhile, Ravi remained behind bars, and seeing that he stayed there was the job of the federal prosecutor, Morris Crump. He was relatively young for his position, and had only recently been hired by the Justice Department. Assigned to prosecute Ravi, many grumbled at having a novice on such a high-profile case. But Crump was smart, aggressive, and eager to do battle in court. And why not? A conviction would secure him a bright future in politics, not to mention a place in criminal court history.

So, let Morris Crump present all the incriminating evidence he wanted.

We had the phone.

Let him bring a hundred witnesses to testify against Ravi.

We had the phone.

And when the prosecution rested its case, one tap on Harley's touchscreen and Ravi would be vindicated.

Alec and I had teamed up to assist in Ravi's defense, and our first order of business was to show his lawyer that all-important mobile device. I arranged a meeting with Mr. Hampstead, and was off to pick up Alec at the VA. But as I pulled up to the curb, I felt a sudden attack of anxiety. My mind flashed back to the time we were last alone in my car. That was the day I nearly drove Alec to suicide.

Alec climbed into the passenger seat, and I immediately felt awkward in his presence. After extending a cordial "Hello" to each other, we drove off.

Our trip was quiet for the first mile or two, then Alec said, "Amy, about what happened that day, I'm—"

"Don't say it! It was all my fault. Your reaction was totally understandable. I just didn't know how to handle the situation."

"You did nothing wrong. *I'm* the one who screwed up. You were my friend that day, and I showed my gratitude by hurting you. Forgive me for being such an ass."

He could have easily accepted my apology, but didn't. I was moved by his honesty, and wasn't about to let him accept all the blame.

"Fair enough," I said. "I'll forgive you under two conditions: One, that you forgive *me* the same amount, and two, that we put that whole thing behind us. You know? A clean slate."

"A clean slate!" Alec held out his hand to close the deal. I hesitated to take it. There was still a lingering fear of his touch that I couldn't quite get past. But he waited patiently. And when I finally shook his hand, I squeezed hard to show him that I was in control. His grip was every bit as firm. We were equals again.

We arrived at the lawyer's office bright and early. A preliminary hearing had been set for the following morning, and we didn't want to take up too much of Hampstead's time. The hearing was of vital importance. It's where the opposing parties meet to present their cases. If the judge feels the evidence is strong enough, he will proceed with a trial.

"Please, have a seat," said the perfumed secretary. "Mr. Hampstead will be right with you."

The wallpaper covering the reception area looked like bookshelves full of law books. Photos of Hampstead handing fat checks to his ecstatic clients were displayed around the room. I squinted at the images to see how large the amounts were, but the checks were blurred out.

Inside Hampstead's private office, we found the lawyer sitting at his desk, his suit coat slung over his high-backed executive chair. His potbelly bulged through his vest as he looked over some legal documents. On the wall behind him were more photos of him shaking hands and grinning.

"Come in, come in!" he said, peering at us over the top of his reading glasses.

Alec and I sat down in the chairs facing his desk. I was just close enough to the lawyer to make out the heading on his papers: *The People vs. Ravi Hakeem.*

Hampstead lowered the documents and let out a sigh. Raising his glasses to his forehead, he leaned forward and said, "I'm not going to beat around the bush. It doesn't look good for Ravi."

"How so?" asked Alec.

"The prosecution has more than it needs for a conviction. The fact that Ravi hid potential bomb-making materials is irrefutable. The money the cops found on him indicates complicity. What have *we* got? No corroboration of Ravi's whereabouts the night of the attempted bombing. Sworn statements from the people on his client list say they've never heard of him. And—let's be honest—what jury is going to acquit a Middle Eastern immigrant accused of terrorism? I'm sorry, but without more substantial evidence, we'll have no choice but to enter a guilty plea."

I promptly stood up. "I've got all the evidence you need—solid proof that the police are holding the wrong man." I held up the device. "This is the phone that was used to call me that night. The files on it show that Ravi did *not* make that call. It was made by a man named Harley Fink."

Hampstead raised his eyebrows. "Harley Fink? Let me see that."

I turned on the phone, swiped to the call record page, and passed it over to Hampstead. The lawyer lowered his glasses and examined it closely. He mumbled a few times, then said, "No. This won't do. Data on digital devices are too easily altered. The judge will never allow it."

He rapidly tapped the screen.

"What are you doing?" asked Alec.

"Tampering with evidence is a criminal offense. Best we delete this data right now."

Alec lunged forward and grabbed the device from the lawyer's hand, but he was too late. The screen was blank.

"You idiot!" yelled Alec. "You've ruined everything."

"I just did you a big favor," said Hampstead.

"Those calls would have cleared Ravi of a capitol offense. Now, no one will know the truth."

With his hands behind his head, the lawyer leaned comfortably back in his chair. "I know what I'm doing. Believe me. It's for your own good."

While they argued, I glanced up at the wall photos and saw the face of Harley Fink in one of them—shaking hands with our lawyer!

"You mean, it's for *your* own good!" I said.

I elbowed Alec and pointed to the chilling photo. Alec pushed his chair away and threateningly stepped around the desk.

Hampstead leaped behind his chair. "See here, boy! Keep your distance! Take one more step and I'll have the both of you thrown out of here."

Alec ripped the photo off the wall and hurled it across the room. "You *want* Ravi to lose!"

"Ravi's discoveries must never be known. There are powerful business interests and political forces at work here. They'll break you and anyone else who stands in their way. For your own safety, I advise you to stay out of it."

"And I advise you to hold on to your nose, because it's about to be flattened."

I grabbed Alec's arm. "That won't be necessary," I said. "Ravi's shampoo will be known soon enough. I happen to know that the FDA is already testing samples of it, and will be announcing their approval any day."

The cocky lawyer laughed. "You sad, little girl. Our man at the FDA intercepted those samples months ago."

Now, I was the one who needed to be restrained. "You won't get away with this! I'll take the stand in court and expose your whole rotten scheme."

"And who will believe you? Without Harley's phone, your story is no better than a fairy tale."

The office door opened and two burly security guards stood in the doorway. Hampstead waved them inside. "Be so kind as to escort these young people out of the building, won't you?"

Alec and I left without any further incident, but not before Alec had one last word for the crooked lawyer: "By the way, you're fired!"

Visiting hours were nearly over by the time Alec and I reached the jailhouse. We had come to update Ravi on the day's disastrous events.

Only phone visitations were permitted between visitors and high-security inmates. That meant that we had to speak to Ravi through telephone handsets, while viewing him through a bullet-proof glass partition.

I had already told Ravi about finding Harley Fink's phone, and how it was going to make winning his case a slam dunk. That was a mistake. My big mouth had raised his hopes for an early release. Now, I had to tell him not to bother packing.

A door opened beyond the glass, and into the secure area stepped Ravi. He spotted us across the room and waved the moment the guard unlocked his handcuffs. My heart ached seeing him clad in his jailhouse uniform. That orange outfit was intended for outlaws and thugs, not for my friend.

Ravi's ankle chains scraped the floor as he shuffled over to his seat. His eyes were bright with optimism. He was happy to see us, but I knew his joy would soon give way to disappointment.

We all lifted our up phones and put them to our ears.

"Look at you two!" said Ravi excitedly. "I was afraid I'd never see you together again."

"All water under the bridge, Dad," said Alec. "You're looking well yourself. How are they treating you in there?"

"No time for chit-chat. Did you see Hampstead?"

Alec and I rolled our eyes over at each other, neither of us wanting to deliver the bad news.

"He's not your lawyer any more," said Alec. "That sideshow phony showed us his true colors, and we didn't like what we saw."

I expected Ravi's radiant face to dim, but his smile only got broader. "No matter. I expected as much. I've already spoken with the judge and he's going to let me represent myself."

Either Ravi's time behind bars had affected his judgment, or he just didn't realize the gravity of his situation. Ravi was a smart guy, but he was no legal eagle.

"Handling my own defense will be easy," said Ravi. "With Fink's cell phone for evidence—"

"It's over, Dad!" blurted Alec. "The phone can't help us anymore, and that was our whole defense."

Ravi chuckled behind his hand.

"Why are you laughing?" said Alec. "That prosecutor's going to nail you to the wall. There's no way you can win."

Ravi rapped his knuckles on his forehead. "You always were a little wooden-headed. There's *always* a way, provided you have the good sense to devise a backup plan. Ever hear the story of David and Goliath?"

Alec stared up at the ceiling with a "now what?" look on his face.

"We know the story," I said. "The little boy defeats the colossal giant. You're David and the prosecutor is Goliath. But there's one thing you're forgetting: the biblical David had a weapon. He had a slingshot."

"That he did," said Ravi, "and proved that sometimes the simplest methods can bring down the biggest brutes."

It all sounded like a lot of rambling nonsense to me. But as always, Ravi's enthusiasm was catching.

"What can we do to help?"

"Is my shaving mug collection still at the shop?"

"No one's touched it," said Alec. "Why?"

"Go and get it. Find a big sack and take all the mugs out of the case, but first put one of them aside: the one on the 3rd shelf, the 3rd mug from the left."

"What do you want with that?"

"It's my slingshot!"

A big guard came and stood over Ravi. Visiting hours were over.

"Bring it with you to the hearing tomorrow," Ravi said, as the guard grabbed the phone away from him.

Back in handcuffs, Ravi was escorted to the exit. But before leaving, he turned back to us and shouted, "3rd row down, 3rd from the left!"

Chapter 15

The Hearing

*T*hink of a preliminary hearing as the first act of a stage play. The setting is a somber court-room. The characters on stage include lawyers, security guards, and, of course, a crusty old judge. The odd thing about this play is that it has no script. The performers make up their lines as they go along. Anything can happen. How the story will end, nobody knows.

The plot is pretty easy to follow. The opposing lawyers each present evidence to support their claims. The judge examines it, and if he likes what he sees, a trial is ordered. But before that can happen, the prosecutor needs to show "probable cause." If he fails, the case is dismissed and the accused walks free. Otherwise, the stage will be set for Act II: Trial By Jury.

Putting on a live show is pointless without an audience. By law these hearings are conducted in open court. That means that anyone can attend. Farmers, financiers, and floozies are all welcome. Alec and I were among the spectators, as Ravi's hearing was about to get underway.

At the prosecutor's table sat Morris Crump, flanked by two assistants. Stacks of file folders and hundreds of documents were laid out in front of them. At the defendant's table, however, there wasn't even a yellow legal pad. Instead, there was a plain paper bag, containing the shaving mug Ravi had asked for. The court bailiff had carefully inspected the item before allowing it into the courtroom. A bomb-sniffing dog even took a whiff of it.

A hush fell over the room as a side door opened. In walked Ravi in handcuffs, with a guard on each arm. A third officer carried in a brief case and some law books. At least Ravi was allowed to abandon his jailhouse getup for a suit and tie.

Released from his shackles, Ravi took his place as his own defense attorney. He looked haggard and weak, like he hadn't slept in days. Then, he saw the paper bag. Peeking inside, his face lit up like a stage light. He scanned the gallery. I rose to my feet and waved. Alec stood, too, giving his dad a big thumbs-up.

"All rise!" ordered the bailiff. "Court is now in session. The honorable Judge Jenkins presiding."

Whispers immediately spread among the observers. Horace Jenkins was notorious for being a hard-ass judge. Handing down stiff sentences for petty infractions was his idea of justice. His callousness had earned him the nickname, "Jail Time Jenkins."

The scowling judge banged his gavel, then addressed his audience.

"For those who are unfamiliar with these proceedings, this is not a trial. It is a hearing. You are here to observe. Do to the sensitive nature of this case, you may feel the need to sound off. I'm telling you right now: Don't! If I hear any outbursts, or see any protests of any kind, the perpetrators will be ejected from my courtroom. I hope that is clearly understood." He lifted his gavel. "This hearing will come to order."

Bang!

Act I: The Hearing

"Mr. Crump?" said Judge Jenkins. "Opening statement, please."

The prosecutor straightened his tie and approached the podium. "May it please the court—"

Bang!

"Don't! Don't! Don't!" roared the judge. "I hate that ridiculous 'please the court' phrase. Anyone using it for the remainder of this hearing will be held in contempt."

Crump cleared his throat. "Your Honor . . . in the case of *The People vs. Ravi Hakeem,* the defendant is accused of attempting to commit a terrorist act on U.S. soil. The prosecution will present evidence proving that Mr. Hakeem:

1. Planted a bomb at The Wild Things Survival Fund offices.
2. Evaded arrest by leading police on a high-speed pursuit.
3. Knowingly hid bomb-making materials at his place of business.

The judge nodded in agreement. "Does the defendant wish to respond?"

Ravi leaped to his feet. "Your Honor! This whole thing is nothing but a witch-hunt. I haven't done anything illegal. The prosecutor is trying to put me on trial to further his own political ambitions. I am totally innocent of all charges."

"Mr. Hakeem," the judge said smugly, "this court is not interested in your innocence or guilt. We are here to consider evidence pertaining to the allegations stated in the formal complaint. If you want to play Perry Mason, do it on your own time."

Ravi slowly sank back into his chair. "Yes, sir . . . Your Honor."

I wouldn't say that Ravi had already lost his case, but he was certainly heading in that direction. Not only was he battling the most ruthless prosecuting attorney around, he was clueless of courtroom etiquette. And if that wasn't bad enough, the judge didn't like him.

"Mr. Crump," said Jenkins, "Is the prosecution prepared to present evidence?"

"Yes, Your Honor. I submit the following documents as People's Exhibit A: The defendant's public record."

Odd that he would bring that up, because Ravi's record was spotless. He was born to naturalized parents. He got high marks in school clear through college. As a local business owner, he belonged to the Chamber of Commerce, and volunteered at Lyons Club benefits. He had no criminal arrests, voted patriotically, and paid his taxes on time. By all accounts, Ravi was a model citizen. There wasn't one word of anti-American rhetoric in his record that Crump could use against him . . . or so I thought!

Crump held a page high up over his head. "This document comes from the U.S. Immigration and Customs Enforcement Agency. It states that Mr. Hakeem's father was engaged in criminal activity in his native country. His crime involved the illegal poaching of endangered wildlife. To escape prosecution, he immigrated to the U.S., but was later captured and deported back to his homeland. There he was tried, convicted, and imprisoned—all of this thanks to the cooperation of the animal rights group, The Wild Things Survival Fund!"

I shot a glance at Alec. He shook his head, seeming as baffled as I was.

Crump continued. "The prosecution contends that Mr. Hakeem—harboring a deep hatred toward this organization—attempted to bomb its headquarters for its role in his father's deportation. Therefore, I move that Exhibit A be admitted as evidence of his guilt."

The judge glared at Ravi. "Objections?"

Ravi shaded his eyes in shame as he rose. "I remember very little of my father, Your Honor. I was a boy when all this happened. But the sight of him being dragged from our house in the night, and the screams of my mother begging for mercy, this I will never forget. But I have since come to terms with that. My father had broken the laws of man and nature, and was dealt with accordingly. I hold no grudges toward any organization, especially one that only wants earthly creatures to live as God intended. I did *not* try to bomb that building. Mr. Crump is trying to twist my boyhood anguish into a motive for committing violence. His evidence is purely coincidental, and I object to him trying to make it appear relevant."

The judge thought for a moment—a very *brief* moment. "Objection overruled! The People's Exhibit A is hereby admitted."

Jenkins might as well have pronounced Ravi's sentence right then and there. Crump had dropped the bombshell he needed to secure a conviction, and the judge wasn't about to stand in his way.

"Does the prosecution wish to offer further evidence?"

"The People's Exhibit B: The report on the FBI investigation."

Again, Crump held all the cards. The report confirmed the chemicals taken from the shop to be common bomb-making ingredients. The police acknowledged finding Ravi's business card at Harley's crash site. There were photos of the raid, sworn statements from eyewitnesses, and transcripts of Ravi's interrogation—all of it portraying him as an evil villain.

Unless he had a miracle up his sleeve, Ravi was done for.

"Objections?" the judge asked him.

Ravi sighed. "Your Honor, I was home asleep the night of the bomb threat. It's a lame alibi, I know, and I don't expect you to believe it. Those materials were used for harmless research. You're not going to believe that, either. So, at the risk of looking stupid, I'm going to object to the admission of the FBI report."

"Objection overruled! The People's Exhibit B is hereby admitted."

Given the judge's reputation, his ruling was not

unexpected. But now came Ravi's turn to show some proof of his own.

"Is the *defense* prepared to present evidence?"

Ravi approached the podium, but this time he stood tall. Confident. "I am indeed!" he said. "The Defendant's Exhibit A: Testimony from an expert witness. With the court's permission, I call to the stand—"

"This is inappropriate," interrupted the judge. "Save your witness for the trial. This court is only accepting *written* affidavits."

Ravi opened one of his law books and turned to a bookmarked page. "According to The State Code on Preliminary Hearings, rule 562 states: 'In the event testimony cannot be taken by deposition, witnesses shall be examined orally in court, as provided in section—'"

"Alright!" conceded the judge. "But I want to know the nature of this evidence."

"The prosecution has tried to portray me as some kind of mad scientist. The fact is, my research is solely intended to benefit the public welfare. I can prove that those so-called 'bomb-making' materials were only used for humanitarian purposes."

"Very well. You may call your witness. But, no TV courtroom dramatics, is that clear?"

Ravi turned toward the gallery. "I call to the stand . . . Amy Dawson!"

What? Me? I was there to observe the hearing,

not to participate in it. But as I slumped down into my seat, Alec nudged me out into the aisle.

Standing in the witness box, I swore that I would tell "nothing but the truth," then took my seat.

"Please state your name," said Ravi.

"Amy Dawson."

"How old are you?"

"Sixteen."

"What is your occupation?"

"Right now I am—or was—a receptionist at the 2-Bit Solution barbershop."

"As an employee, were you aware of a science laboratory on the premises?"

"Yes. That's where you mix up your magic shampoo."

The spectators chuckled.

Judge Jenkins folded his arms. "You're trying my patience, counsel. Get to the point."

Ravi resumed. "When you say 'magic' shampoo, can you be more specific?"

"I'm talking about the magical properties in the Guilt Remover."

"And what does this Guilt Remover do?"

"Well, when you shampoo your hair with it, all your feelings of guilt are washed away."

Laughter filled the courtroom.

Bang!

"Order!" cried the judge. He leaned down to me. "Young lady, do you know what it means to be under oath?"

"Yes, sir. It means if I tell a lie, you'll throw me in the pokey."

"Well put. Then, perhaps you meant to say that you read about this magical shampoo in a fairy-tale—that guilt-removing haircare products don't really exist."

"That's not what I meant at all. Not only *does* it exist, I've had my own hair washed with it."

"Mr. Hakeem!" spouted the judge. "This testimony is utter nonsense."

"With your permission," said Ravi, "I wish to ask the witness one final question: Will she please describe her experience using this shampoo?"

"Very well, I will permit the witness to respond, but remember, young lady . . . under oath."

I looked out at a roomful of bewildered faces.

"Have you ever done something really stupid that you later regretted? Well, that's what I did. I hurt someone I cared deeply about. I didn't mean to, but by then the damage had already been done, and nothing I could say was going to *un*do it. The guilt I suffered was more agonizing than I can say. That's when Ravi gave me his special hair treatment. As the shampoo soaked into my scalp, I drifted into a kind of dreamlike state. That's when the change happened. I realized the fact that nobody's perfect. That people make mistakes. I was suddenly free of all guilt, as if my shame had simply melted away. And as I awakened back into the real world, a voice inside me said, 'You can live with that, now, can't you?'"

The courtroom was dead silent. No one—not even Judge Jenkins—uttered a word. Then, a voice called out from the gallery:

"Where can I get some of that stuff?"

"I want it, too!" cried someone else.

"Do you take Visa?"

In a matter of moments the courtroom erupted into near chaos. People shouted and shook their fists, demanding to know where they could obtain the miracle solution.

I lost count of how many times the judge banged his gavel. "This is my final warning," he screamed. "One more outburst and I will clear this courtroom!"

As the bedlam subsided, he turned to the prosecutor. "Do you wish to cross-examine the witness?"

"I wish to *object!*" hollered Morris Crump. "This testimony is erroneous and misleading. A magic shampoo, if there is such a thing, is irrelevant to this case."

"But it *is* relevant," argued Ravi. "Explosives can be made from household items, yet you don't see the FBI arresting housewives with bathroom cleansers. Just because those chemicals were in my possession, doesn't mean I was making bombs with them. This testimony sheds reasonable doubt on the prosecution's claim of malicious intent."

"The defendant is turning this court into a fantasyland. The witness' claims are absurd. There is no way to prove this shampoo does anything more than wash hair."

Judge Jenkins jotted down some notes, then said, "The court rules that the existence of a guilt-removing shampoo cannot be substantiated. This evidence is therefore declared *inadmissible,* and I order the witness' testimony permanently stricken from the record."

All eyes were on me as I returned to my seat. Though my speech had moved the spectators, it failed to soften the hardened heart of the judge. But the final scene of this courtroom drama was yet to be played.

"If you won't allow testimony," said Ravi, "then I submit Defendant's Exhibit B: *Physical* proof that the Guilt Remover is real."

He grabbed the paper bag and approached the bench, then pulled out its contents: a novelty shaving mug with the gavel for a handle.

"*This* is your exhibit?" joked the judge. "Does the prosecution have any objection to admitting a shaving mug as evidence?"

Crump whispered in the ears of his assistants. After a quiet snicker, the lawyer said, "No objection."

The judge examined the mug while trying to keep his own laughter in check. "I hate to tell you,

Mr. Hakeem, but if this is all the evidence you have, I'd say your defense has gone down the drain."

"Not down the drain," said Ravi, "into a bucket." He unscrewed the hollow base of the mug. Hidden in a secret compartment was a small vial of clear liquid.

"What have you got there?" the judge asked nervously.

Ravi displayed a wicked grin. "You thought I wouldn't remember you, but I do. You came to my shop back when you were a young criminal prosecutor. You used your gift for persuasion to send a man to prison, knowing full well he was innocent. Your guilt was so great that you begged me to remove it—which I did. And here it is!"

He uncapped the vial, reached across the bench, and poured the liquid guilt into the judge's water glass. "Go ahead, judge. Take a sip. All your gut-wrenching regret will be restored to you—or do you still maintain the Guilt Remover isn't real?"

The judge hastily chucked the glass into a wastebasket. "Restrain this man!" he ordered.

The guards quickly subdued Ravi. He offered no resistance as they slapped the cuffs on him. But despite his humiliation, the hearing wasn't over.

"Your Honor," said Ravi, "I believe I'm entitled to make a closing statement."

"I'll give you one minute."

Not a pin-drop was heard as Ravi composed

himself. He looked down at the chains clasped tightly around his ankles.

"Finding sympathy isn't easy, is it, judge? When did forgiveness go out of style? We've all done things we're not proud of, but why should bearing the weight of that guilt be a life sentence? The Guilt Remover was created so that the unforgiven can live a guilt-free existence. You may be a high and mighty judge, but I've learned something you haven't. When compassion enters our hearts, wonderful things happen. We become human again—more merciful, more tolerant. I believe that all people, regardless of their shortcomings, deserve to be treated with an equal measure of kindness. Can you say the same?" He turned to the gallery. "Can any of you?"

But the cold-hearted judge was unmoved. He addressed the courtroom.

"Regarding *The People vs. Ravi Hakeem,* in the view of this court, probable cause has been sufficiently established. The defendant will thereby stand trial in federal court, and will be bound over without bail until a trial date is set."

It's been said that our legal system doesn't guarantee justice, only a *chance* at justice. If that's true, then Ravi was the most unlucky man in the world. Act I of this drama was over, but I was proud of Ravi's performance. He battled his adversaries bravely. He spoke passionately from the heart, but in the end, the play's antagonist would have the last word:

"This hearing is closed."

Bang!

Chapter 16

Be Gone

"We'll be right back after this commercial message," said the late-night talk show host. The live TV audience applauded, as the band launched into a lively tune.

This is the ad the home viewers saw:

```
FADE IN:

            ANNOUNCER
   Attention! The following
   message is for anyone suffering
   with severe guilt.

INTERIOR - OFFICE CUBICAL

MAN sits at his desk. Tense. Can't
keep his mind on his work.

            ANNOUNCER
   Is a guilty conscience getting
   you down? Are you losing sleep
```

over an honest mistake? All
your life you've tried to be
fair, thoughtful, and decent.
Now, every morning you wake to
that nagging guilt. Well, don't
sit there feeling sorry for
yourself.

MAN looks up into camera.

                    ANNOUNCER

Wash away your guilt with
Guilt-Be-Gone!

A shampoo bottle magically *pops*
into MAN'S hand.

                    ANNOUNCER

Introducing the amazing shampoo
that guarantees you guilt-free
living.

                                    CUT TO:

INTERIOR - SHOWER STALL

Bare-chested MAN in shower.

                    ANNOUNCER

Simply apply Guilt-Be-Gone
instead of your regular
shampoo. Lather, rinse, and
watch your shame go down the
drain. Its scientific formula
not only cleanses your
conscience, it leaves your hair

healthy and manageable. Plus,
it's sulfate free and
environmentally safe.

                          CUT TO:

Close-up on product.

                ANNOUNCER
Guilt-Be-Gone works on all
sins, from evil deeds to the
slightest indiscretion:

    Deceit
    Infidelity
    Fraudulence
    and More!

You could spend thousands on
antidepressants. Psychotherapy
can cost even more. But Guilt-
Be-Gone won't cost you $5,000
dollars. It won't even cost you
$500 dollars. Right now,
through this incredible TV
offer, Guilt-Be-Gone can be
yours at the unbelievably low
price of only $499.95.

But wait! Be one of the first
100 callers and receive a free
shampoo dispenser. Call in the
next 10 minutes and we'll send
you a second dispenser
absolutely free! That's a $5
dollar value!

CUT TO:

INTERIOR - OFFICE CUBICAL

MAN is back at his desk. A
flirtatious young secretary walks
by and winks at him. He smiles
back at her, then gives the camera
a thumbs-up.

ANNOUNCER

Guilt-Be-Gone is not available
in stores. Quantities are
limited. Operators are standing
by. Call now!

FADE OUT

That was all it took! Snipper Jim had answered
the call of a guilt-ridden nation. With one airing of
that commercial, he scored enough orders to clear
out his entire inventory. By dawn he and his crew
had packaged, labeled, and shipped every last bottle.

The lowly hairdresser had made himself a small
fortune. To hide his taxable income, Jim's earnings
were deposited into offshore bank accounts. All of
this was illegal, of course. Aside from dodging the
taxman, Jim was peddling stolen goods containing
substances not approved by the FDA.

But the shampoo's safety wasn't a concern to
Jim's buyers. Media coverage of Ravi's hearing had
everyone craving the miracle product. Not even its

exorbitant price deterred ordinary people from getting their own bottle. The rich and powerful—who really needed it the most—hoarded it by the case.

The minute Jim's crooked operation was uncovered, police were dispatched to his hair salon. What they found was an abandoned building. The empty back room revealed evidence of a hasty retreat. Barber chairs, hair dryers, and beauty supplies had all been left behind. The only clue pointing to Jim's whereabouts was an airline ticket receipt to a foreign destination.

Needless to say, none of Snipper Jim's profits made it into Ravi's pocket. Languishing behind bars without bail, no amount of cash was going to get him out of there anyway.

Having his life's work sold on the black market upset Ravi terribly. He fell into a deep depression. He wouldn't eat. He wouldn't speak to anyone. He became so despondent that the police placed him under a 24-hour suicide watch. As weird as this may sound, that was the best news I had heard, because that evening . . .

A security guard making his rounds discovered Ravi's jail cell empty. There were no physical signs of escape. The cell lock hadn't been jimmied open, nor had the bars been pried apart. Ravi simply wasn't there.

The police scoured the jailhouse grounds. They

combed the backwoods by helicopter. Road blocks went up. Homes were searched. They looked everywhere—all the while scratching their heads, wondering how their prisoner had escaped.

But Ravi's vanishing act was no mystery to me. It was a brilliant backup plan. Anointing his head with Guilt Remover provided him the perfect means of escape. All he had to do was think suicidal thoughts, and *whoosh,* he'd be transported from the jail to the barbershop mirror. And I would be there to welcome him.

Alec gripped the dashboard as I raced my little car through the night. "Slow down!" he demanded. "A speeding car is just what the cops are looking for."

"But if they get to the barbershop before we do, they won't let us near it, let alone go inside."

"Use your head. The police are already there. The shop is the first place they would have gone to look."

Somehow, I imagined that rescuing Ravi would be like a Sunday walk in the park. We would leisurely stroll into the shop, apply a little Back Splash to Ravi's noggin, then make a clean getaway. At least Ravi was safe. No policeman in his right mind would search for an escapee in a mirror.

To appease Alec, I let up on the gas. But as the car began to slow, we heard the wail of sirens behind us. Red and blue flashing lights lit up my rearview mirror. I reached for my car registration as I pulled over, certain I'd be issued a speeding ticket. But our pursuer didn't stop. The vehicle following us wasn't even a police car. It was a convoy of fire engines.

"That's a break," said Alec, as the big red trucks zoomed past us. "Now, let's keep it down to a safe speed, shall we?"

But instead of easing away from the curb, I jammed the car into gear and floored the gas pedal.

"No time for that," I said. "Look!"

Down the road ahead, plumes of smoke billowed into the sky, as an orange glow flickered against the downtown buildings.

"Dear God!" cried Alec. "It's the shop!"

A crowd of onlookers gathered to watch the fiery spectacle. Helmeted firefighters in yellow jackets scrambled in all directions. High-pressure water hoses, bulging like well-fed jungle snakes, criss-crossed the street. I raised my arms to shield myself from the intense heat, as Alec and I entered the surreal scene.

Flames had already engulfed the barbershop's ground floor. Spreading to the upper level, the upstairs windows exploded from the blistering heat. Despite the best efforts of the brave firefighters, the blaze raged out of control.

My feeling of helplessness was overwhelming. There must be a way in there, I thought, but the unyielding flames guarded every door and window. And as I watched the walls crumble, I knew that all hope of saving Ravi was lost.

I saw the horror in Alec's eyes as he stared at the blaze. Somewhere inside that raging inferno was his father—perhaps dead, perhaps trapped in an alien world for all eternity.

I slipped my hand into Alec's. His tearful gaze stayed on the flames, as he gave it a gentle squeeze.

A familiar voice called my name. "Amy!" Hubert, too, had followed the trail of smoke in the night sky.

"I'm so sorry, Amy," he said.

"Please don't be. Things like this happen, that's all."

"But this was no accident. I overheard the investigators say that it was arson. A real professional job. They'll probably never catch the guy who did it."

Hearing that disturbing news, Alec dropped my hand and ran toward the shop. Shoving aside spectators and firefighters, he stopped at the front entrance. Bursts of flames roared out through the doorway, as if taunting him. A fireman pulled Alec back, yelling, "It's no use, son!"

Struggling with the fireman, Alec finally relented, tearfully falling to his knees in defeat. He staggered to the other side of the street, then sat on the curb and buried his head in his hands. Hubert and I went over to him, but neither of us could find any words of comfort.

As I lay my hand on his shoulder, Alec tipped his head up. "So, on it goes," he said, gazing at the shop's smoldering remains. "There are two kinds of people in this world: those who take, and those who take *more*. When will it ever change?"

Most of the fire trucks had gone, leaving a few firemen to watch over the hot spots. What was once the 2-Bit Solution barbershop was now a huge mound of charcoal. With his home and family destroyed, Alec would soon be off in search of new horizons. What lay in store for him I could only wonder. As for me, my incredible journey had come to an end.

"Nothing more to do here," said Hubert. "Can you give me a ride to my truck?"

Alec and I drove him down a side street to his SUV. Hubert climbed out of my car, then opened up the rear liftgate of his truck.

"Anything you guys need?" he asked.

"Nothing. Thanks."

"Not even this?"

He reached in and pulled out a heavy object: a large, round mirror—*Ravi's* mirror!

"There was no one around when I saw the smoke pouring out of the shop. I called 911, then broke down the front door. I had just time enough to yank this off the wall before the flames got to it."

Hubert lowered the mirror to the ground. Amazingly, a pair of eyes peered over the frame in the reflection. A face then timidly rose into view. It was Ravi, still in his orange jumpsuit!

With his hand on top of his head, he grumbled, "Try being a little more gentle with this thing."

"Relax, tough guy," said Alec. "We'll have you out of there in a jiff." He held his hand out to Hubert. "I'll do it."

We turned our attention to Hubert, but he just stood there.

Alec snapped his fingers. "The Back Splash, please."

Hubert silently stared at the ground.

Alec's face turned pale. "Don't tell me!"

"There wasn't time," confessed Hubert. "I when back for it, but . . . I'm sorry."

We had fought a noble battle, and were so close to victory. We had outsmarted the police, survived a deadly fire, and found Alec's dad unharmed. But without that key to Ravi's freedom, he was no better off now than back in jail.

Ever the optimist, Ravi took it all in stride.

"Don't worry about it," he said. "Look at it this way: Hang me on a wall and I'll make the world's greatest conversation piece. Or, how about the bathroom? Put me over the sink and we can chat while you brush your teeth."

Ravi was trying to cheer us up, but it wasn't

working. Then we saw a dark shadow move across the mirror. We weren't alone. Behind us stood an unfamiliar figure.

"Will this help?" asked the stranger.

If I never believed in miracles, I did now. The intruder was Debbie Fink, holding a bottle of Back Splash in her hand!

"Where did you get that?" I asked her.

"My dad swiped it from the shop years ago. He was a thief, even back then."

"No," said Ravi. "I *gave* it to him. He kept it for me in case of just such an emergency."

I leaned over Ravi. "You mean, you trusted that snake?"

"Debbie probably doesn't remember, but her dad and I were close friends at one time. We nearly became business partners. I was good at imagining, and he was good at selling. How was I to know he'd turn against me?"

"That's easy," said Alec. "You took away his guilt. He could then be as cruel as he wanted and never feel sorry for it."

Debbie stepped forward and lifted her bottle, like raising a glass of fine wine. "All I can say is, if this isn't an emergency, I don't know what is." She twisted off the bottle cap. "Anyone for a shampoo?"

The TV was on in our living room, as I quietly tweaked the front door closed. Due to the lateness of the hour, I planned to sneak upstairs to bed before anyone saw me. After all I had been through, the last thing I wanted to hear was, *Where have you been?* or, *Do you know what time it is?*

I could have easily gotten away with it, too. Dad was sunk into the living room couch, absorbed in a TV newscast. The rest of the household was likely fast asleep.

But I decided I was beyond such childishness. I walked in on my dad, as if everything was hunky-dory. To my relief, he quickly glanced over at me, then said, "Did you hear about the big fire tonight?"

Now that the pressure was off, I could have simply wished him a good night and scampered off to bed, but I didn't.

"Come watch," he said.

Normally, I would have sat in the comfy armchair, but I felt the need to sit next to him.

Realizing he was getting special attention from me, he asked, "You alright?"

The newscast was playing video of the raging fire at its peak. Bystanders were interviewed, each describing the blaze as if the end of the world was coming.

I bowed my head and folded my hands, like a Sunday school pupil. "I was there," I said. "I was at the fire."

Dad reached for the remote and clicked off the TV. I prepared myself for a lecture, but instead, he asked calmly, "Do you want to tell me about it? It's okay if you don't."

I looked up at his concerned face. "No, I *want* to talk about it. I want to tell you everything."

I started out slowly from the beginning, describing my first day at Ravi's shop.

Dad listened attentively.

I spoke of police raids and talking squirrels.

He nodded politely.

I told him about jumping over rooftops of condemned buildings.

He raised an eyebrow.

Dad remained remarkably patient, even after I explained how people pop in and out of mirrors.

I ended my story by saying, "I'm sorry if I worried you."

"I wasn't worried," he said. "Ravi has been keeping me updated."

"How do you know him?"

"He called. Employers have to get parental consent before hiring a minor."

I was stunned. "So, you knew what I was doing the whole time."

"Well, not the *whole* time."

"What about all that talk about letting me spread my wings?"

"I want you to have that freedom. But, even a tightrope walker needs a net under him while finding his balance. I wanted to be there to catch you in case you fell. I was just being a responsible parent. You wouldn't want a slacker for a father, would you?"

In a million years, I wouldn't wish for *any* other dad, but I couldn't tell him that—not yet, anyway. That would be like telling him that I loved him—which I did. Don't ask me why, but there's an awkwardness that always crops up at moments like these. But, it's okay. Feelings like that don't need words put to them. Just knowing they're there is enough.

"I'm curious," said Dad. "What made you decide to open up to me?"

"I don't know. I should have told you what I was doing all along. I guess keeping it to myself made me feel . . . guilty."

"How do you feel now?"

"Better."

"Better than if you'd used the Guilt Remover?"

A little giggle snuck out of me. *"Way* better."

I let out a yawn and rose from the couch. Dad switched off the lights and grabbed a late-night snack from the kitchen. I locked the front door and closed the blinds. At the top of the stairs, a warm bed and a soft pillow were waiting for me. I breathed in the quiet.

"Night, Dad."

"Night, sweetheart."

Chapter 17

Giving Back

"*A*re you watching?" said the voice on my phone. The last time I heard that question I was asked to watch a televised police pursuit. Again, I was instructed to tune to a TV news channel. This time it was a live press conference from the White House.

The U.S. President stood at the pressroom podium, as reporters fired questions at him. The issues raised were all fairly typical: When are you going to fix the economy? What are you doing about climate change? Who was that woman we saw you with last night? There was nothing to suggest that we were in the midst of a national crisis. So, what was so urgent that I had to sit through this tiresome Q & A?

Though terribly bored, I'm glad I did, because what happened next was anything but dull. While the president responded to rumors of his misconduct, his hair suddenly turned . . . *white!*

It just popped on, like switching on a light bulb. It happened so fast that no one knew how to react. At first, gasps spread through the press corps, then giggles. Unable to see his own hair, the president thought he had unwittingly told a joke. "What?" he said. "What did I say?"

With that, the whole room erupted into laughter. "Is George Washington's hairstyle coming back?" joked one reporter. But before the befuddled president could reply, the secret service whisked him out of the room.

News cameras panned over to capture the reporter's expressions, but their smiles didn't last long. One by one, *their* hair started turning white, too. Print journalists, TV newscasters, foreign correspondents. *Pop, pop, pop!* It was like watching popcorn bursting in a stove top popper. Those who were unaffected either poked fun at their colleagues, or hightailed it out of the room, fearing they would be the next victims.

For sure, it was a moment not to be missed. But, who was that calling to let me in on the joke?

"Who is this?" I asked my anonymous caller.

"In a minute. Turn to channel 7."

At the New York Stock Exchange, investors celebrated the end of the trading day. A group of them happily rang the closing bell and applauded another round of excess earnings. Shrieks then rose from the trading floor as their hair turned snow-white.

I saw the same thing happen on other channels. C-SPAN showed congressmen with their hands on their bleached heads running from the Senate chambers. A basketball star's dreadlocks turned white as a floor mop while shooting a 3-pointer. A reality cooking show suddenly went black when the hair of its judges turned frosty.

"This is awesome!" I told my caller. "But, who *is* this?"

"Don't you recognize my voice? Maybe this will help: Yoooou Maaaake Meeee Smiiiile!"

Only one person had ever sung that tune to me. "Ravi! Where are you?"

"I probably shouldn't say. I'm still considered an escaped criminal, and as we both know, phones can be bugged."

"What's with all the white-haired people? Are you doing it?"

"Thank Snipper Jim. Those drums he stole from me *didn't* contain Guilt Remover. They were filled with peroxide, mixed with a special time-release agent of my own creation. Jim's TV shoppers thought they could erase their guilt without anyone finding out. Well, now they've got some serious explaining to do."

"Peroxide? Why would you do such a thing?"

"It was only a matter of time before my discovery fell into the wrong hands. So, I decided to conduct a little experiment. By turning their hair white, all the guilty people would be exposed. I expect you'll hear a lot of apologies in the coming days. But the real test will be in how the rest of us respond. Many will want to ridicule them, but a lot of us won't. You rarely see it these days, but I believe people have a hidden desire to forgive, if given half a chance to show it."

"What about all that Guilt Remover? You must have had a thousand gallons of it in storage."

"I destroyed it—and every drop I had left over. When I saw the trouble it was causing you, and the toll it was taking on everyone else, I decided it wasn't worth hanging on to. And just as well, I say. It's time people resolved their own hang-ups without some silly shampoo to do it for them."

I was talking to a defeated man. He had devoted a lifetime to improving our quality of life, and for what? The very people he tried to help were the ones who brought him down. He had lost his home, his business, and all his possessions. But Ravi didn't sound disappointed. He actually sounded happy.

"Is there anything I can do?" I asked.

"You've done more than your share already," said Ravi. "I think Alec would agree with me."

"Isn't Alec with you?"

"Didn't you hear? He's in Colorado Springs training with the U.S. Paralympic running team. He finally got his act together. He wrote off Duke's Place once and for all. Those battlefield flashbacks are now little more than a nuisance."

"So, you *did* find a cure for his PTSD."

"Indeed I did, but it didn't come out of a bottle."

"Then, what cured him?"

"*You* did! He hid in the shadows until you shoved him out into the sunlight. You reminded him that while there is ugliness in the world, its beauty is worth living for. What he needed wasn't a miracle solution, just someone to reintroduce him to life. You did that, Amy, and I'll be forever grateful."

Who would have thought? Out of the ashes of Ravi's defeat would rise the victory he had so wished for. Alec, too, would rise to become a world champion, and revel in honoring his country in a positive way.

"Where does all this leave *you*," I said, "especially with the police on your tail?"

"They won't be after me for long," said Ravi. "I fully expect to have all charges dropped, as soon as I give the District Attorney his guilt back. A drop or two of it in his lunchtime cocktail ought to do it. Meanwhile, I'm putting everything back the way it was. After all the years I've held on to my client's guilt, I think it only fair I return it to them."

"How many vials have you got left?"

"Only a few hundred or so," he said, laughing. Then I heard police sirens in the background.

"Looks like I'd better be on my way. We'll meet again, someday, Amy Dawson."

Then he hung up.

Well, I was feeling pretty special after all that. I had earned myself a good night's sleep. I moved my new book from my bedspread to the end table. It was titled, *And Then There Were None*—another Agatha Christie classic. The story centers on a group of murderous socialites. Plagued by guilt, each one is found murdered under mysterious circumstances. Don't you just love good fiction?

As I climbed into bed, Scraps jumped up and laid his head on my lap. He tilted his head back and I scratched behind his ears. It was a ritual that played out every night at bedtime. With his eyes half-closed in ecstasy, he looked at me as if asking, "Am I in heaven?"

Ravi promised me a lap dog and he certainly delivered. His anti-aggression shampoo had turned a savage beast into a gentle pet. Too bad the rest of the world couldn't have benefited from Ravi's genius.

But then, Ravi wasn't like everyone else, and being accepted when you're different doesn't come easy. If only people could be more like me and my dog. We shared a mutual respect for each other's uniqueness. Scraps showed me his by keeping my lap warm, and I showed mine by keeping his food dish full. No anger. No bitterness. No tears.

As my cozy mutt drifted off into Doggie Dreamland, my phone rang again. This time it was Hubert.

"Did you hear about Z Beanie Run?" he said. "He decided that with all the millions he earns from record sales, his concerts should be free. I guess his guilt from ripping kids off was too much for him. Anyway, I'm going to his show tomorrow night." A long pause. "Wanna come with me?"

The nerve! He was asking me out again, knowing full well how I felt about dating friends. There was only one thing left for me to say:

"I can't think of anything I'd rather do more."

About the Author

Bruce Edwards was born in Marin County, California and raised on a tasty diet of jazz and Disney animation. He majored in Architecture in college, but switched to Music to join the burgeoning San Francisco music scene. As a composer and musician, he wrote rock tunes and radio jingles, and toured as a pop music artist. He tinkered with early computer animation which led to a career as a feature film character animator. His more unique vocational detours included a stint as a puppeteer and performing magic at Disneyland. As a writer, he wrote screenplays during his Hollywood years before finding an audience for his young-adult fiction. Mr. Edwards lives in Orange County, California.